The Christmas Cookie House

The Christmas Cookie House

JENNIFER GRIFFITH

For Andrea

Chapter 1

Leela

Leela Miller tugged at the hem of her shirt, rolling a loose thread between her fingers. The metal folding chair's chill seeped through her pants into her legs. The library smelled like old books and too much perfume.

Sitting there, in the seat that had been Mom's for a dozen years—up until life and fate had dictated otherwise—Leela was filling her vacancy but not the void. Leela could never do that. No one could.

But she at least had to try. Getting into the Ladies' Auxiliary would be a perfect place to start.

Una Mae Coldicott had the floor, and something she said caused an uproar, jerking Leela from her thoughts. "And so, with Greta Green bowing out at the last minute"—she shot a deadly gaze at Greta, who sank in her folding chair—"I'm afraid several drastic changes will have to be made for this year's major fundraiser."

No chairwoman! How would the Cookie House fundraiser happen without someone to steer the ship? Poor Greta. It must have been something serious. Greta was looking at her shoes, her face redder than Santa's coat. Who would step in and chair the event?

"In fact, we may have to cancel it and use what's left in our coffers from years past to fund our service projects for next year."

A gasp rang out, bouncing off the high ceiling of the old library and back again for another go-round the group. Double gasp.

No chairwoman was one thing, but *no Cookie House?*

"We can't cancel it outright, Una Mae."

"Well, unless one of you steps up …"

A glance played hot-potato around the group. No one wanted to bite off something that huge. Not this late in the game. Not this close to the holidays.

"It's a shame, considering this is the first Christmas since Freesia Miller's passing, but …"

Una Mae let out a dramatic sigh, and all the blood drained from the top half of Leela's body.

The first Christmas without Mom, and now Mom's big contribution to Massey Falls was getting the axe! Leela curled inward.

It's like Mom is dying all over again.

"Canceling the Cookie House is too drastic, Una Mae." Mrs. Imrich stood up. "If the Cookie House doesn't happen, all our future service projects go into jeopardy."

Leela looked around. Everyone was upset but no one was as jarred as Leela, who felt like a bomb had exploded right next to her, dulling her senses.

The room blurred, as did all the ladies' voices. The back of Leela's stomach rumbled, like an oncoming avalanche. Leela was going to do something rash—right in front of all the ladies of the Ladies' Auxiliary meeting—right in front of Una Mae Coldicott, their queen.

"Excuse me?" Leela was on her feet, interrupting Una Mae who was running at the mouth. "I'd be willing to serve as chairwoman for the Cookie House."

Every Aux lady in the room stared wide-eyed at Leela's novice outburst.

Leela was tearing at the seams. "I'm up for it. I have lots of ideas."

Not true, but to keep this event alive, she'd get them.

"We could try again at Valentine's Day." Una Mae went on as though Leela hadn't interrupted. "Greta, you'll be in better shape for chairing by then, I assume."

No. Leela couldn't let that happen. "It's a Christmas event. It's tradition. I can do this."

Una Mae's eyes crinkled at the sides, and not in good-natured charm. "You?" Was it just Leela, or did the syllable drip with poisonous sap? "You haven't even been admitted to full membership, Miss Miller, nor have you served your probationary year."

"I practically grew up in the Ladies' Auxiliary." And Leela would have applied for membership before now, if she'd been living in Massey Falls. *I should have been living here.* "Maybe chairing the Cookie House could serve as my induction requirement."

"Induction requirements are more along the lines of finding five local businesses to donate to the event," Greta Green said, "or making ten batches of cookies for the fundraiser instead of five—not chairing the whole thing."

Leela's gaze darted to the faces of the board members. Some of them looked skeptical. Others looked at her like she was their savior. No one wanted to chair this monster at the last minute.

"Give her a chance, Una Mae," Mrs. Philbert insisted. "After all, her mother, God rest her soul, was the original founder of the Cookie House idea."

Murmurs erupted. Discussion skittered across the surface of the room.

Una Mae slammed her gavel on the wooden block. "Order!"

All talking hushed. Una Mae leveled a gaze at Leela that could have stopped a freight train.

"I may be a novice"—Leela pressed away the quaver from her voice—"but so much is already in place from years of tradition. The date, the third Tuesday in December, is set in stone. The bakers, the logo for all the advertising, the relationships with the community. Greta

Green did a great job bringing us to the top of the ninth inning." Leela gave Mrs. Green an apologetic smile. "The venue is set and lovely."

This last phrase's flattery might be transparent as a window to Una Mae Coldicott. This year she was slated to again host the Cookie House at her historic mansion on Society Row.

"All the engines of the ship are fired up. Don't we just need someone at the helm to steer it into a successful harbor?" *Please say yes, and please let me into the group.*

"I move we vote," Mrs. Imrich said. "As we have no other candidates, and Leela Miller is willing to put in the time, I think we should approve her."

Una Mae Coldicott's voice would have curdled milk. "I'm sorry. It turns out my home will no longer be available to host the event."

Of all the cruel, last-minute switches!

"Why not, Una Mae?" Mrs. Philbert put both her palms on the table. "It's been at your house for the past five years."

"That was one of the contingencies I stipulated when I announced that Greta Green had bowed out."

"But the ads have been designed with your address."

"I'm sorry. I trust Greta implicitly to keep my home and its possessions secure during the event. This volunteer"—she said the word like it was covered with barbed wire—"hasn't exactly put in the time required to earn such trust. I'm sure all of us feel the same about the sanctity of our homes."

More murmurs erupted, while the rug that had been beneath Leela's feet ripped the rest of the way out, and she fell back into her folding chair with a metallic clunk.

No. No, no, nope.

Leela needed this assignment too much to let a location change stall her.

"I'll secure a venue."

"Like your home?" Una Mae lifted a sneering eyebrow. Could eyebrows sneer? Una Mae's could.

"My house isn't large enough." Nor was it on Society Row. Nor was Daddy in any state to have his familiar world rearranged. That wouldn't be fair to him. "But I have an idea." Leela didn't. "Trust me, please? I'm sure you'll all agree it's very important to keep the Cookie House tradition alive."

Una Mae hadn't completed her decimation, however. "There's another factor to consider. I've just come from a meeting with the Winterfords. They'll not be available to host the Holiday Ball, either."

No venue for the Holiday Ball! The sister event to the Cookie House always happened the same night, and was also hosted at the home of an Aux member.

"Hey, now, Una Mae. That wouldn't fall under the responsibility of the chairwoman of the Cookie House." Mrs Imrich had a grumble that was contagious. "And what's wrong with Eileen Winterford? Why would she back out now? And why isn't she here?"

"Ed's decided to drag her off to Sun City," someone whispered in a gossipy tone. "He's forcing her to be a snowbird."

"The event is a whole day affair. We can't deliver either day or night at this point. Our only choice is to cancel."

Leela gulped. Maybe she'd bitten off too much. "This is the chairwoman's problem to solve," she heard herself say. Una Mae didn't blink. "I can do it, if you'll let me."

Mrs. Imrich wedged her way into the showdown. "Let's say she solves it." She turned a kind face to Leela. "Do so, and you'll be inducted—with no probationary year. It's a big deal, as you know."

"Yes." Una Mae's voice could have curdled cream. "Fail, and you disgrace the Auxiliary and leave us penniless."

Leela grinned the way a cartoon character did when faced with a dragon, sweat beading on her brow. "I'll make it happen. I'll get a venue that will be perfect for both events."

Una Mae sniffed. Mrs. Imrich called for a vote.

Leela was approved. She exhaled, but then the breath caught. How on earth was she going to do this?

5

I may have just sealed both my membership rejection letter and the death notice for Mom's legacy.

Unless ...

There was exactly one house in Massey Falls that might work. Not that it was owned by a member of the Ladies' Auxiliary, so that lengthened the shot even more. But it was gorgeous and spacious and, as far as rumors went, currently unoccupied since Jingo Layton had passed away.

The meeting broke up. Leela charged out into the snowy day, texting Emily.

Want to do some window-peeking?

Which was how she found herself and Emily both peeking through the side window of Society Row's newly vacant Layton Mansion ... and breaking it.

Chapter 2

Jay

Jay Wilson slid the key into the lock of the old Victorian mansion. The door creaked open, and turpentine fumes wafted from all the stripping of finishes Jay had done since inheriting the house from Uncle Jingo.

Also—sawdust, new paint, and drywall patch scents floated from the thousand other projects to bring it back to life.

"Looks worlds better," Burt Basingstoke's voice boomed. "Best real estate flip of the decade. That is, if you decide to list it."

Oh, Jay was listing it, all right.

With the winter sunlight coming through the windows, the Layton Mansion looked good, if he did say so himself. Looked like a pro had done it, and not a mere recent-veterinary-school-grad.

Not bad at all.

"You sure? Now that you've officially brought it out of decrepitude"—Burt slapped his hands against his thighs, and snow scattered onto the hardwoods—"you could at least enjoy it for Christmas. You're invested in the place."

Truly invested: blood, sweat—and a lot more sweat.

"No, I have definite plans for the proceeds." Jay wiped a line of dust off the top of the chair rail above the deep mahogany wainscoting of the historic Layton Mansion. "I've been offered a partnership buy-in at a small-animal veterinary clinic, Precious Companion."

Doctors Foster and Cody were taking a big risk on him, new grad, and Jay wasn't going to let the chance slip by—not if he could secure the funding.

"Precious Companion. Over in Reedsville, eh?" Basingstoke didn't sound impressed. But he should have. A partnership at a practice straight out of vet school was a big deal. "Small animal vet though, right?" Burt smirked.

Jay never should have mentioned to Burt his preference for large animal veterinary medicine. "Are there any comps for this house to know how much we should set as a list price?"

Jay needed his sweat equity to pay off. He'd put in as many hours a day on the house as he had studying for his veterinary boards these past few months.

"Let me show you some numbers." Basingstoke punched a calculator on his phone, then flashed the screen at Jay. There floated a range of possible sales prices, all of which covered the buy-in at the clinic. The higher end would even pay off a huge chunk of his student loans, too.

Jay gave a low whistle. "Nice."

Uncle Jingo Layton had given him the best graduation gift of all time—he'd potentially set up Jay's finances for life.

"Sure, sure. But why not set up shop here in Massey Falls? Dr. Harrison, the local vet, only works on horses. All of Massey Falls has to lug sick cats a two-hour drive each way, over the hills, and on slick roads this time of year."

"I'd like to stay." Sort of. Well, not really, but how to put it tactfully? "There's just not enough business in a town this size." A town with more horses than dogs. Certainly not enough population to provide him the income to pay back all the money he'd borrowed for veterinary school. Not *and* set up a practice.

"When do you find out about your boards?"

"Actually, the email came this morning—I passed!" Not to brag, but passing veterinary boards was a serious accomplishment.

"Officially licensed!" Burt high-fived him. "Way to go, son."

"Thank you." Years of work were finally, *finally* paying off. His career goals were so close now he could almost smell the cat food. His post-student life could officially start. Maybe he could even find someone—and quit being a lonely fool with his nose in the books all day long.

"But Reedsville? Are you sure? I mean, think about it, Jay, before you commit. You do already have a house here, free and clear. Could you commute?"

Too far.

Besides, Reedsville was a much better place for a single guy his age. In a town the size of Massey Falls, fat chance finding anyone to date.

Basingstoke wasn't dropping his suit, though. "This house would be a good place to raise kids." Basingstoke knocked on the wood. "The banisters would be fun to slide down, anyway."

"Yeah." But not enough to give up the chance of a partnership at a thriving clinic.

Pity, since with the sun streaming in, the floorboards gleamed. And Jay would miss out on ever lighting a fire in the grate of that master bedroom's adjoining parlor. Refinishing in there had been a labor of love to see it go from gaggy to gorgeous.

"The client is always right." Burt clapped loudly. "So! That means we'd better get this house on the market right away. Chop-chop!" He did an air-karate-chop.

"Chop-chop." Exactly. "I agree because—what if I told you I have a New Year's Eve deadline?" Foster and Cody weren't keeping the partnership offer open indefinitely. They had a slot to fill.

"I'd tell you *no problemo*. Rumors have leaked about the Layton Mansion possibly coming on the market. Buzz is buzzing." Burt grinned the grin that said *I'm the source of those leaks and the cause of that buzz*. Smart business. "Several buyers have expressed interest."

"Several?"

"It's the Layton Mansion. It's on Society Row, the toniest street in Massey Falls. Even though it's been shut up for years by Jingo, public interest in its mysterious inner workings has never faded."

Public curiosity, eh? That could work in Jay's favor. Frankly, the inside had been nothing but a hoarder's paradise when he took over his mom's childhood home. With all the junk wedged in every crevice, it'd been hard to believe there was ever room for his mother to be raised in this place. Uncle Jingo couldn't have even fit a pet in here.

"That's encouraging."

Burt lowered his voice, leaning in. "It's still in the works, but I may even have a few cash offers lining up." Burt straightened his spine like he'd just delivered game-point at Wimbledon. Then he curled his fingers, blew on them and rubbed them against his lapel.

"Cash means fast transaction, right?" Jay knew book-loads about osteopathic surgery on pets but little about buying or selling property.

"You betcha. Cash is king. These buyers really got excited when I hinted that a cash sale would mean they could occupy before Christmas. Roaring fire, stockings on the mantel, all of that."

Hee-haw! "What's holding us up? Let's list it today." The first week of December cut it close already, considering how long he'd heard it could take to close. Of course, with a cash offer, that could go quicker, and Jay could be out of here and treating canine ringworm before Dasher and Dancer and Prancer and Vixen's takeoff time.

"Good. Good! Okay, then. Let's just double check you've finished all the stipulations from Jingo Layton's will."

Again? But Jay had already nearly worn out the knees on three pairs of jeans refinishing floors in the sprawling three-floor brick mansion. "I've done everything on the requirement list, plus the back parlor's hearth." And the gaggy-to-gorgeous project hadn't even been on the list. He'd refinished that out of respect for the meticulous woodwork.

"Ah, no. Not quite." Burt snapped the latches on his briefcase and pulled out a sheaf of papers.

"Seriously? There's more?" Besides that hearth, in addition to rewiring all the electrical and replacing all the lead and clay pipes with modern plumbing, he'd gone over every inch of the place with sandpaper and wood stain.

He'd removed wallpaper.

He'd ripped out old carpet and restored the original hardwood floors.

By sheer force of will, he'd ripped out the cabinets, appliances, and plumbing.

He'd upgraded kitchen and baths to a beautiful, modern standard.

This place was finished. D.O.N.E. *Finished.* In the process, he'd grown to love and hate it at the same time.

"I need to list it, Burt. The clock is ticking."

Burt looked up from a document. "Great. So, you just need to accomplish the final requirement, and I'll line up a buyer."

Jay bit back a growl. "The last requirement being …?"

"The attic. I thought we'd been over this. You have to clear out the attic."

Attic! Jay slapped his forehead. How could he have forgotten the attic? Probably because he'd *wanted* to forget the attic.

In truth, Jay hadn't even been up there to check it out. It might be cramped, or huge, he had no idea. Maybe cleaning it out would be fine, no problem, easy fix.

Hoarders hoarded on their main floors and not their attics, right?

It would probably be fine.

Okay, this could be very bad.

Don't let your worries show, man! Be cool.

"Easy. I'll have it done by nightfall if you can get one of those roll-off dumpsters over here for me. There's probably a dormer window up there I can use. I'll jettison every box and junk trunk through the window, straight into the trash."

"Not so fast." Burt dragged his finger down the side of the paper

11

from the file. "Trashing isn't an option."

Burt spouted legalese so pointed it hurt Jay's eardrums, but Jay got the gist: before Jay could post the house for sale, the contents of the attic must be inventoried.

Inventoried!

That, and they must be made available to any other surviving relatives of Jingo Layton. Well, that list would be comprised of Jay and his mother. Ceri Layton Wilson, a.k.a. Mom, had sworn never to set foot in Massey Falls or the mansion ever again.

"You're sure redoing the whole downstairs isn't sufficient?" Jay didn't mean to sound ungrateful. This one property sale could erase most of his student debt. He could start out his career at the vet clinic in Reedsville at a net zero. What new doctor could say that?

Still, he seriously didn't want to clean out a hoarder's attic.

Burt checked the time on his phone. "Look, Jay. Or, I should say, Dr. Wilson. I'm heading out to meet another client. I like what you've done down here. It's top quality work. We can get the official listing up right away—as soon as the attic is done to Jingo Layton's specifications."

Jay wasn't getting out of doing the attic. "Okay. So, timeline-wise, do you think tomorrow afternoon is a reasonable expectation?"

"I've been up there." A low chuckle escaped Burt Basingstoke's throat. "Word of warning, son. It's not going to be a one-man job. I'd advise hiring someone to help you. That, or make a friend. I know you're fairly new around here, but getting help is the only way you'll be done before New Year's. Trust me."

A friend. Around here? Jay had barely met anyone other than clerks at the hardware store.

"Besides. If you had a friend, maybe we could induce you to stay in Massey Falls." Burt tugged his scarf tight against his neck. "Think about it, Jay. The Layton Mansion ought to have a caretaker with Layton bloodlines."

Oh, brother. Local guilt-pressure. Just what he needed.

Burt left in his big luxury sedan, and Jay eyed the stairway to the next floor, which he would have to climb to examine the attic, and—

Crrrack! Something cracked, crackled, and thudded on the grand ballroom side of the house. Raccoons? Foundation settling? One of the yard's towering elm trees damaging the entire roof? It could be anything. Jay broke into a jog to check on the source of the sound.

Blast it! If this house fell apart now, he'd never get it sold in time.

Chapter 3

Leela

Leela Miller lay on her back in a pile of brambles outside the Layton Mansion. Thorns stuck through her coat sleeves and down under her scarf, pricking her neck and throat. Poking around here without permission had been a huge mistake. Twenty-five-year-old women did not window-peep.

Her bare hand gripped the splintered two-by-four of the window frame, onto which she'd been hanging for balance while peeking in the window. Turned out it wasn't the Rock of Gibraltar she'd needed. In fact, now it was more the Matchsticks of Gibraltar, and she was officially a vandal.

Couldn't the wintry sky all just fall down on her? A hollow laugh of despair rang from her throat. This wasn't happening.

"Oh, Leela! We broke the Layton Mansion!" Emily tugged Leela to her feet with the strength and vigor of her sixteen-year-old enthusiasm, and Leela brushed dried rose leaves off her coat. "I'm so sorry. I should have held the firewood log steadier so you could look inside the window, not let it wobble and tip you into the roses. I'm so sorry."

Leela shouldn't have asked Emily to hold a log in the first place. Making a younger cousin a partner in crime was wrong on a lot of levels. She gripped what was left of the broken window frame. What was she supposed to do with it? Splintered wood didn't repair well. Or disguise well, either.

"Well, despite this misfortune"—she wielded the board—"I did see inside."

Emily dropped the log, which she'd hauled back to the woodpile. It clunked. "You did? Are there chandeliers?" She came running back to Leela's side.

"The whole ballroom had them. And ceiling medallions."

"I swoon for a ceiling medallion." Emily threw herself back and made a snow angel. "Oh, I really hope the new owners let you use it for the Christmas Cookie House! They just have to!"

No kidding. If only the owners could instantly see how important the event was to the town—and to Leela. "Especially after my rash, irrationally exuberant promise to the Ladies' Auxiliary this morning. There isn't anywhere else that will work. Not in this amount of time." It was the Layton House or nothing, now that Una Mae had yanked her own house.

"What about Yuletide Manor? I thought Natalie was your best friend *and* your roommate."

"They've got two family weddings booked the day of the bake sale." Leela had called Natalie first—and Natalie had apologized, even offered to try to reschedule the weddings. Of course, her baby was almost due, and Leela couldn't pile on more stress. Plus, they were *family* weddings. There was no treading into those waters. "It's the Layton House or …" Or failure.

"So, correct me if I'm wrong, Leela." Emily waved her arms up and down to make the angel's wings. "The deeper reason we're here is because you enraged the president of the Ladies' Auxiliary when you refused to go with her lecherous son as his date to the Holiday Ball, right?"

"Pretty much." Una Mae had had it out for Leela ever since Leela turned down the date invitation. Maybe before, but Leela couldn't point to why.

"You were smart to say no." Emily shuddered. "If I were you, I'd rather chew rocks than be stuck in the talons of Felix Coldicott all night, listening to his lewd suggestions. I hear he collects spiders. To feed to frogs. Which he then feeds to … I'll stop, but the pattern continues."

Now Leela shuddered. "Felix isn't my type. That's for sure."

"She can't exactly hold you personally responsible. Doesn't Una Mae *know* she's raised a pervert?"

"Probably." Which was probably why Una Mae must be desperate to get the guy a date to the high-profile event—and why she'd be willing to hold her own historic home for ransom until Leela capitulated. Which she wouldn't.

Because somehow Leela was going to track down the new title-holder of the Layton Mansion and get him to let her use it for the Cookie House and the Holiday Ball. The place had a ballroom, for Pete's sake. It screamed *solution!* for her dilemma.

There had to be property records or something she could research to get a name and address for the owner.

Leela helped Emily out of her snow angel, careful to keep it intact, with no footprints inside the lines. An angel would never have a muddy footprint on her dress or sleeve.

"I don't suppose you could ask your dad to find out who owns this place?" Leela asked as Emily brushed snow from her jeans. "He knows about all the properties in town." Leela's cousin-in-law Burt Basingstoke knew his business.

She probably should have gone to him first, actually, because trespassing like this, and breaking stuff was a criminal offense, and—

Footfalls pounded toward them, almost squeaky in the freshly fallen, moisture-heavy snow. "Is someone out here?"

It was a man's voice.

They'd been caught trespassing! Or else someone was there to attack them. Attacks were unheard of in Massey Falls, but still, women couldn't be too careful. Strangers without their hometown values could wander through town and prey on unsuspecting girls.

Leela stared down at the splintered wooden board in her hand. The possible weapon of defense grew to a thousand guilty pounds, but she gripped it hard. Just in case.

The man appeared around the brick corner of the house. "Who's here?" he asked again.

Whoa, there, Comet and Cupid. What choir of heavenly angels had deposited that guy in this town? Dark hair and eyes, a perfect build, and a voice that could melt butter. She reached for the side of the house to steady herself. But she missed, and toppled into the brambles again. Whoops. She popped to her feet.

"Hi. Were you interested in the house?" he asked, looking Leela over. His gaze landed on the broken window frame above her head, and then down at the board in her hand.

She chucked it into the brambles. Yeah, she'd get that later.

"Interested! Obsessed is more like it." Emily laughed nervously at Leela's side.

"Hey. Yeah, sorry." Couldn't Leela melt into the snow? "We, uh, were just trying to get a look inside."

"If you want that, I have a key to the property." He must be the real estate agent. Rumor-mongers around town had whispered the mansion would be coming up for sale soon. "You didn't have to sneak."

From the brambles the broken board screamed an accusation. *You are a vandal. You broke the house!*

"Heh-heh. Sorry about that." Leela rubbed the back of her neck. Blast it. She was apologizing too much. "Little mishap."

"Um …" Emily tugged on Leela's coat sleeve. "I think I'd better go tend my brother's puppies." Emily dashed, stepping right in the center of her snow angel. She sped like a hare down the sidewalk toward her Society Row house a few doors down.

Cowardly accomplice. There were no puppies at the Basingstoke house.

"I will repair it."

"That won't be necessary, Mrs.—?"

"Leela Miller. Miss, not Mrs." Oh, geez. Was she flirting? If so, she was really out of practice. Why was her neck getting so hot? She didn't even have her scarf on. "Please let me make it right. I don't want to be someone who breaks something and leaves." Not ever.

"Why"—he raised a flirty eyebrow—"exactly did you break it, may I ask?" Well, he could ask all day if he kept flashing her that alluring grin.

"When I'm not busy breaking people's window frames, I'm helping the Ladies' Auxiliary plan their annual fundraiser by looking for a last-minute venue. Our original locations fell through this morning." *Possibly my fault, but also not my fault one bit.*

"Venue?"

"The Layton Mansion would suit the event so perfectly." Gorgeous, right on Society Row, great for the curious minds of Massey Falls—plus, the ballroom! "It has always been my favorite house in town. It's a lot of people's, in fact."

"But I heard old Jingo Layton never let anyone inside. How could it be a favorite of yours? Or anyone else's?"

"Based on curb appeal, I guess. And vivid imaginations." At least that was true in Leela's case. "I've been imagining Christmas mornings by the fire in there for years."

Uh, what mischievous inner-elf had possessed her to admit that?

"Yeah," Jay craned his neck up toward the third story windows. "Uncle Jingo did have a hermit-hoarder thing going on." The dormers were dark up there. "I'm Jay Wilson, by the way." He stuck out his hand, and she shook it.

"Nice to meet you." Holy amperage, Batman! Leela had encountered lots of handsome customers while working at the bookseller's shop back in Reedsville and nothing like this near-electrocution handshake had ever occurred. "If you know the new owners, would you ask them about letting the Ladies' Auxiliary use the Layton Mansion for the Cookie House this year?"

"The cookie what?"

"Cookie House. Huge Christmastime fundraiser? Annual event. Famous, really. Surely you've heard of it."

"I'm picturing a giant house out of gingerbread." Clearly, he hadn't heard of it. "I mean, I like gingersnaps. They're my favorite, but there's a limit to how much gingerbread can be appreciated at once. A whole house of it, well ..."

Seriously? No. No way. How could someone expect to sell real estate in Massey Falls and not have heard of the Cookie House? It was like living in New York City and not hearing of the Macy's Thanksgiving Day Parade.

Leela would help the guy, give him the lowdown on it, and then maybe he'd help her get in touch with the new owners of the Layton Mansion. Quid pro quo here.

"Listen, Jay. You need to know about this event or you'll never succeed in Massey Falls. Trust me. Massey Falls *is* the Cookie House and Holiday Ball." Which, as a prospective member of the Auxiliary, she'd have to attend. Probably stag. Humiliating. "Be there or be square, as they say."

Jay did have a killer square jaw. So square might be acceptable, in his case. Even admirable. *I am such a nerd.*

"Good to know. My mom grew up here, but I'm a newcomer."

Well, his mom, whoever she was, hadn't done Jay any favors by not cluing him in on the most important cultural aspects of Massey Falls. Leela would have to fill in the gaps in his education. After all, he was cute—if electrically dangerous—and she'd hate to see him make a fool of himself in town before he even got started on his real estate career.

"Then I'll give you a Massey Falls insider tip." How could she convey the appropriate level of importance to him? "The Ladies' Auxiliary does all the community's major service projects year-round. They provide eyeglasses for the elderly. They keep up the landscaping flowers at Garson Park. They deliver meals to the home-bound." Including to Dad now and then. Which probably killed him, to some degree, every time Mrs. Philbert's minestrone appeared.

"That's noble." Jay sounded unimpressed. A breeze wafted the scent of soap and peppermint off his person. Mmm. He smelled clean.

"All those activities take funds, and the Cookie House is how they pay for them. Everyone in the community comes and buys cookies—at generous prices—from a beautifully decorated historic home."

A home like the Coldicott Mansion, usually. Fussy and decorated to the hilt with Christmas kitch. Last year, Leela had heard, Rudolph the Red-Nosed Reindeer had been a star player, and they claimed Una Mae had saved all the Rudolph stuff for a repeat.

Except not this year, thanks to Felix and his unwelcome attentions to Leela. The guy's last three girlfriends had been exotic dancers, for pity's sake. Leela, with her barely kissed lips and former bookshop manager résumé, was *not* his type.

And vice versa.

Jay seemed to be considering. "Well, the Layton Mansion isn't what I'd call beautifully decorated. It's bare. No one lives in it now."

"All the better. Then we won't have to store furniture to make room to display cookies." In fact, with an empty house, they could display exponentially more cookies. The Layton Mansion could make this the best year for the fundraiser ever. "I really think the community would turn out in force if the new owners would allow us to use the Layton Mansion for the event. You'll talk to them for me, won't you? It's for such a good cause."

Her eye fell on the busted window frame. She'd wrecked the place. She wasn't bargaining from a very strong position. In fact, her position looked a lot more like kneeling and begging.

He had to say yes that he'd help her. He just had to.

Chapter 4

Jay

Jay couldn't peel his eyes off this Leela Miller girl. It wasn't just because she had the most stunning blue eyes, or that she had a whole bird's nest of rosebush leaves poking out of her light brown hair. It was more the sincerity of her plea, and the goodness of it.

So noble. And gorgeous. And what was up with the second he'd touched her hand? Zappo. Could static even build up when a person walked through snow? Unless it had nothing to do with static and everything to do with Leela Miller's electric touch.

Too bad he couldn't help her. At least not by allowing a huge event like a fundraiser to delay getting the Layton Mansion on the market. Basingstoke was using the enticement of taking occupancy before Christmas as a lure for cash buyers—which made sense. Families didn't want to move during the holidays, and they'd want a gorgeous Victorian mansion, with its large hearth and high ceilings for a giant Christmas tree, to be part of their holiday memories the first chance they could get.

And getting new owners in meant good things for Jay, too.

This pretty-eyed girl's Cookie House thing could totally interfere, no matter how noble.

"When is this shindig?" he asked anyway.

If he'd thought Leela's eyes were bright before, they went up by a thousand lumens now. "Are you saying you'll help me persuade the new owners? Oh, Jay! I knew from the second I saw you, you were going to be important to me. I mean—to helping me with the Cookie House."

He noted the slip-up and flattered himself with it for a brief moment, even though it couldn't come to anything, since he'd be gone to Reedsville by the end of the month, if the fates allowed.

"The third Tuesday in December. And you won't regret it."

Wait. He hadn't agreed to anything yet. Yeah, and he should tell her he was the new owner. Like, now.

At first, he'd thought she'd been kidding around, acting obtuse about who owned the place, when it was obviously Jay, so he hadn't spoken up. Now it felt awkward, and a little too late. He'd embarrass her if he mentioned it now.

He walked toward the house, fingering the front door's key, and Leela met his pace through the new snow. "You should at least see the inside before you go on requesting the house." Jay shouldn't be doing this. He should just assert a definite no. But he was going to show her his work. *I mean, I went to all the work. It would be nice to share the result with someone who obviously likes the house already.* "It might not meet your expectations."

"Oh, it will meet them, I'm sure." She followed him up the steps to the porch.

"Where do you work, Leela?" Might as well get to know her a little. He fumbled with the key, putting it in the lock—even though he hadn't locked it when he'd gone running to check out Leela's commotion. But he didn't open the door yet.

"I used to manage a bookshop in Reedsville. I'm home now, taking care of my dad full-time."

"Is he all right?"

"Dad taught school for most of my life, but there was an accident. My mom cared for him until a few months ago, when breast cancer took her too young."

"Sounds like quite a year." What hollow comfort he offered. He felt stupid saying anything.

"Tough one. For sure."

Losing her mom. Jay couldn't imagine. Even though his dad had skipped town right after Jay was born, Jay still had Mom over in Torrey Junction.

"You said your mom grew up here."

"Yeah." Right here. In this very house. Jay gazed around. It was hard to think about her here, young, not the struggling person she'd become. For terrible, wrenching reasons in her past, Mom had moved away from Massey Falls as soon as she could jump ship after high school, leaving Grandpa and Grandma Layton and Uncle Jingo behind, barely ever looking back. "She doesn't come back to Massey Falls, though." Enough of this topic. "So, are you saying you gave up your job in the city to start caring for your dad?"

"I didn't have a choice." Leela leaned against one of the pillars on the porch, as if the topic required physical support to discuss. "Dad would have gone into a nursing facility if I hadn't come home. I'm an only child. Yeah, I have a lot of cousins who live around here, but they all have kids and lives. I came home. He's my dad."

But her life! She gave up her job and moved back to *this* place? "Sounds like you're his angel."

"I'm no angel." She smirked, and the twist of her mouth made something twist inside Jay. Too bad she'd come to Massey Falls about the time he was heading to Reedsville, or he could have gotten interested in exploring where that twist might lead.

But he was leaving—by New Year's.

Jay pressed open the front door, holding it ajar for Leela Miller.

"I appreciate your interest in the house, but I have to be transparent with you." He followed her inside. Their footsteps echoed across the hardwood. It smelled like wood glue and hard work in here. "The house is being listed for sale as soon as possible. Sign in the yard and everything."

Leela whirled around to face him, her hands clasped at her chest. "It's being sold? Oh, I wish I could buy it." Her eyes sparked electric blue again. "Well, probably so do half the people in the county."

"That would be nice. The sooner it sells, the better."

"How soon? Not before the fundraiser." Her voice squeaked on the last word, like he was sorely disappointing her.

"The term *as soon as possible* contains one caveat."

"What do you mean?"

"There's a final requirement before buyers can consider it. A home improvement task of possibly gargantuan proportions."

Leela's gaze roved the room. "No way. It looks perfect already. Oh, my jingle bells!" Leela walked the perimeter of the room, mouth agape. She touched the chair rail, crouched to caress the wainscoting he'd backbreakingly restored, and peered at the mantel over the big fireplace. "This finish work is exquisite."

Did she really think so? He'd labored long over the details. *She likes it.* A warm gush flowed through him. She was the first person he'd shown, other than Burt Basingstoke. "Exquisite, eh?"

"This banister!" She flew toward it, caressing the woodwork. "Can you believe how perfect it is? Christmas garland will loop like bunting, and it will be more charming than Donny and Marie, put together."

"That's a lot of charming. And a lot of tooth-whitener." His snark masked how much he basked in her compliments—which didn't appear to be stopping anytime soon.

"Who would have thought Jingo Layton was such a great—I don't know—housekeeper? Look at the sheen of this varnish. That's love right there. I watch a lot of HGTV, so I'm aware of the work involved in a project like this."

"Trust me, it was a ton of work." A lot more than the abridged versions shown on HGTV. "Some of the summer and all of the autumn."

"Wait—who did this work?" Leela stopped, her hand dropping

from the banister's ball. "I mean, Jingo Layton wasn't around this autumn, may he rest in peace."

Jay shifted his weight and glanced down at the dark circles of wood stain which still outlined his fingernails.

"Don't tell me *you* did all this work! Not alone. No. And just so you could list it for sale?" Leela blinked at him, those blue eyes ablaze. "Oh, Jay. From what I hear about Jingo's collecting habits, I bet it was a serious task."

"You have no idea." Every crevice had needed cleaning. Jay had made more trips to the dump than a hungry seagull. "It's a lot better now."

"I think"—Leela reached out and touched his forearm—"you gave it the love it had been missing."

Yeah, maybe he had. "Do you want to see the rest?"

Did she! Leela Miller breezed through every room on the main floor, gently touching the custom touches he'd included in the kitchen, bathrooms, parlor, and ballroom, oohing and ahhing at his handiwork.

How would she like his favorite place in the house? He led her toward the back parlor. Not that he was testing her, but ... was it as gaggy to gorgeous as he believed? "This is the refinishing project I enjoyed most."

"That mantle! Look at the scrollwork! So much effort and skill and love." She grazed her fingertips across the grooves. "I can see why it's your favorite."

It was as if she could sense every drop of sweat he'd shed. "I'm glad you like it."

Leela sighed, and she turned to him with pleading. "With everything you've poured into it, this house is beyond perfect for the fundraiser. Please, can you convince the new owner to let me use it, and *then* put it up for sale? Please?"

The double *please*s hit their mark. He almost said, *sure.*

Why doesn't she know I'm the owner? Hadn't it been a rampant local rumor that Jay had inherited the house from Jingo Layton? He'd assumed everyone in a town the size of Massey Falls would have talked that fact to death.

"I'd better clarify something—"

Her phone rang, interrupting him. She pulled it out and listened, her eyes going from bright to frightened in an instant. "Okay. I'll be there as quickly as I can." She paused on the phone for a second before hanging up with a "Love you, too," and shoving it in her pocket and looking for the exit.

"Everything okay?" Jay followed her long strides across the ballroom.

"Sorry, Jay. It's Dad. I have to go right now—and I didn't even get to see upstairs. I'm dying to see the second floor, especially if there's more room to display cookies." She was almost at the front door now. "You'll call me, right?"

"If you give me your number, I will." For the first time in months, he was asking for a girl's number—albeit under false pretenses. Not awesome, but he'd clear things up. As soon as he got a chance, he'd tell her he'd inherited the place.

But can I let her use the house? I'd have to tell her I'm taking the first reasonable offer. Possibly the first unreasonable one. A quick sale would wreck her plans.

"Here, use this to text yourself. Then I'll text you back later." She shoved her phone into his hand, shifting her weight and glancing nervously at the door.

Jay's thumbs glided over the screen. Then, in a flash of brilliance, he took out his own phone and snapped a photo of her. He captured a half-smile of surprise in the picture—as well as some cute tufts of sticks and leaves. "For my contacts."

"Hey. You gotta warn a girl." She took her phone back. "Please, I'll be waiting to hear from you—about the Cookie House." She hustled out the front door and jogged across the snowy street to a car.

She must not live on this so-called Society Row. Jay stood on the porch watching her go.

Dying to see the second floor, huh? How about the third?

Maybe she would be just the friend he needed to help clean out the attic. He wouldn't mind spending a few hours one-on-one with Leela Miller.

This might work. What would she say to a terrible, dusty project in exchange for the use of the house for her event?

Chapter 5

Leela

"Oh, good. You're home." Emily greeted Leela at the front door of her house. "Your dad's all settled now. Just a temporary scare."

Leela exhaled. "Thanks for being here, Emily. I was caught up in …"

Emily snickered. "In that dreamy guy. No need to pretend."

"We were talking business."

"I'm sure you were." More snickering. A sixteen-year-old was possibly not the best confidant.

"You said Dad fell?"

"Before I got here, don't know how long."

Dang. It could have been as much as an hour. Leela shouldn't leave. Ever. Except that he would want her to be in the Ladies' Auxiliary, as a tribute to Mom.

"I got him back into his bed. Brought him a drink of grape soda." Dad's favorite.

Leela paced down the hallway toward Dad's room, slowly pressing the door ajar. His eyes were closed, and his chest rose and fell peacefully. "Hey, Dad," she whispered. "You all right?"

He must be. He was sleeping. Leela pulled the blanket up a little higher on him, and tucked it near his chin. It was okay. Dad was okay.

"Thanks, Emily. I'm so glad you came and checked on him." *Since Mom can't anymore* was the unspoken adverbial phrase.

"No problem. I love Uncle Frank. We all do." Emily meant it, of course.

He'd built up a lot of goodwill in the family before the accident that had claimed Dad's career, his mobility, and even his voice ten years ago when Leela was a teenager, Dad had been in Mom's care. She'd done everything for him. Now Leela provided the care—with occasional family help.

"Sorry I called in a panic, when he was actually all right."

"No, I'm glad you called." Even though it meant not having a chance to seal the deal with that real estate agent. At least she had his number. Maybe she could pester him later. Er, persuade him.

Emily and Leela returned to the kitchen, and Leela ran the hot water in the sink, adding some dishwashing liquid, the kind that smelled like lemons.

"Come on. Tell me everything. I saw the way he looked at you. What do they say in those romance novels? *He devoured her with his eyes.*"

"Oh, pshaw." Leela unwound her scarf. As she did, the side of her hand caught on something crisp. What was that? Oh, great. A rose leaf in her hair. Nope, make that two. No—three, five, six—Jiminy Crickets!

She tipped forward and shook her head. A full shower of dried rose leaves with spiny edges blizzarded onto the countertop. She swept them into the trash. Oh, brother! What must Jay have thought? That she was a walking, talking tree?

"I'll help you with the dishes if you'll dish."

Dishes from the morning's baking experiment were stacked everywhere. The trash bin contained all the results of Leela's failed sugar cookies—and her failed lemon bars, and misshapen pumpkin roll. Who knew simple cookies could be such a disaster? They sounded so elementary, with their jaunty two-syllable title, *cookies!*

If only she could find Mom's best recipe. It refused to turn up, even when Leela turned the kitchen inside out looking for it.

"Fine." There were a lot of dishes. Leela could use the help. "But there's nothing to tell."

"Come on. I felt the crackling air between you two. You were just complaining there's no one to date in this town. Now you can't say that anymore, unless Mansion Hottie is married."

Married! Well, maybe he was. He'd definitely pried into Leela's marital status, though. That had to mean something.

"We kept things strictly business." Even the handshake, though it had been a lot more like a vacation to the surface of the sun than business. "He's going to talk to the new owner for me about letting us use the Layton Mansion."

Or ... was he?

"But he got your number?" Emily's eyebrows bounced. "I bet he did. I bet if you dropped even a slight hint he would take you to the Holiday Ball."

"Not happening." In fact, possibly none of it was happening. Not without Jay Wilson's help.

"You can't miss the Holiday Ball. You're almost in the Ladies' Auxiliary. They all go. Even your mom went, and she hated that type of thing."

Yeah, Mom had been much more about the cookies and a lot less about the fancy dresses.

"I'll bet you all the frosting on the cookies you'd go if Mansion Hottie asks you."

"His name is Jay Wilson."

Emily giggled like she hadn't heard Leela. "Besides, you have to see my debut!" Emily spun, taking up the whole middle of the kitchen, as if she were wearing a hooped ball gown. "It's going to be so pretty. And I have a date."

She did? Even Emily had a date to the Holiday Ball? Sigh. "You're going to be beautiful. Whether I go to the ball or not, I'll help you with your hairstyle."

"Seriously? That's awesome. But it won't be the same without you actually there." The relentless teen pursed her lips and mouthed *pretty please* a dozen times.

Before Leela could argue, the phone in her pocket chimed, and then chimed again. She dried her hands.

Emily scrambled to her side. "That's a text from him! I know it!"

"It's not going to be him. Come on." An unknown number flashed on the screen. "It's probably a telemarketer. They always want me to sign up for so-called free cruises to the Bahamas if I'll just give my credit—"

Leela, do you have plans for tomorrow morning?

"It *is* from him!" A squeal erupted from Emily, who stood reading over Leela's shoulder. "He's asking you out! I knew it!"—she twirled—"I knew it!"

Leela's mind slipped into the cloud of steam rising up from the kitchen sink. In its billows, she envisioned an outline of Jay's face. That jaw line.

He's going to be important in your life, a voice whispered through the steam. It was the same stupid phrase she'd accidentally blabbed earlier. Which was stupid. Leela didn't know anything about Jay Wilson. He was a stranger.

"You have a date!" Emily swirled in an invisible ball gown.

"It's not a date. It's probably to discuss details of the Cookie House. He's considering it. He's very professional."

"Professionally gorgeous." Emily spun again. "I'm going to check online and see if he's done any modeling anywhere. Jay Wilson, did you say?"

"Stop."

Where had that steam-whisper come from? Leela shivered it away. It lied. It had to be lying. Leela wasn't interested. The guy was probably the type to get restless in a small town like Massey Falls. Jay Wilson would leave.

Like Blaine.

Except Blaine had been cramped in Reedsville, which was ten times the size of this place, and had left after a year. Quick math … a tenth of a year …

Leela gave Jay Wilson five weeks in Massey Falls, max. Good guys left. That was just life. Good guys left Leela.

"What are you going to wear on your date with Jay Wilson?" Emily waved a measuring cup in the air, like she was a fairy godmother conjuring up the perfect date outfit. "I know! That cute red sweater— makes your curves unstoppable. He will turn into a quivering mass of desire."

"You are sixteen! I'm going to tell your mom you're talking like that." Leela wouldn't, of course. But she did steal the dish towel, spun it into a rope and whipped at Emily's leg.

Emily jumped away, laughing, and then took back the towel. "Red sweater, I say."

Leela resumed washing. "Why didn't you tell me your dad had hired someone new at his real estate firm?" Jay had to be with Basingstoke Properties, right? There was only one real estate firm in Massey Falls.

"Aw, I'm a kid, even if I do use terms like quivering mass of desire. Dad doesn't exactly talk shop with me."

Probably true.

"And believe me, he'd *doubly* not tell me if he hired someone gorgeo-licious like that guy. He knows I'd flirt with him." She batted her lashes. Oh, dear. "But don't worry. I know he saw you first."

Well, at least Emily was playing fair.

"Unfortunately." Emily made the sound of a swooning heifer calf. "So what does the second text say?"

Leela dried her hands.

Would you be up for a home improvement project?

"See? It's not a date." Home improvement project did not sound like a date. Or a place to wear a red sweater. More like a shapeless sweatshirt. Though she might get up early enough to put on a few extra swipes of mascara before meeting him.

Helping him out might sway him to talk with the owners. She'd better line up someone to watch Dad and tell Jay yes.

Where? And what time?

Maybe she should ask what the project was, too. But it might sound stingy, and she needed his help.

Crack of dawn at the Layton Mansion. Wear old clothes. You up for that?

Emily dried a cookie sheet from the rack. "Tell him yes. Stop waiting. What else do you have to do? Aunt Sal can watch Uncle Frank while you cozy up with the electric sander and Mansion Hottie." She made it sound sultry.

It wouldn't be sultry. "Jay didn't even explicitly say he'd be there. Besides, I need every minute to perfect my cookie-baking skills before the Cookie House. Or at least to get them up to *edible* condition." Without Mom's recipe, Leela had baked utter mediocrity into every type from macarons to macaroons, from meringues to no-bake cookies. "Thus far, I'm only getting lukewarm results."

"Judging from the contents of the trashcan, they're stone cold, not lukewarm."

"Insult accepted." No one would buy Leela's bakes at the Cookie House. She'd disgrace the fundraiser, devalue it, if she brought something as bad as today's pumpkin spice disaster.

"You're not going to tell him no. Just answer him."

Fine. *I'll be there.* "Gah. I should have sent *See you there.*"

"Rookie move. You should have said *Can't wait to get involved.*" Emily cackled.

Involved. The word hung in the steamy air. Leela hadn't been *involved*, at least not with a guy, in a long time. Not since Blaine, whose empty promises decimated her senior year of college, uprooted her to work at the bookshop in Reedsville, and left Leela with a lot of

Unfinished Everything in her life.

Leela scrubbed harder, her knuckles scraping against dried-on dough. Then she got an idea.

Who all will be there tomorrow? If it's just going to be me and the new owner, I have to admit, I'm a little on edge. Will you be there, too? What if the owner is—

She typed and hit send before thinking. But not before adding *icky?* to end the text.

Icky! She'd just suggested the new owner of the Layton Mansion could be *icky*. Why couldn't she unsend texts? Leela should stick her head in the dirty dishwater and never come up for air.

"What's wrong?" Emily snatched Leela's phone. "Icky? Seriously, Leela? You're hopeless at this flirting thing."

"I know," she moaned. She didn't even argue that she hadn't been trying to flirt. Misery, thy name is texting.

The pile of dishes shrank, with no response from Jay Wilson. How stupid could she be? How insulting? This was his client, and how was Jay supposed to respond?

So much for all her feigned professionalism.

So much for the Layton Mansion as the Cookie House.

Tomorrow morning, she would start walking all through Massey Falls, door to door up and down Society Row, and then branch out from there, begging for someone to let the Ladies' Auxiliary invade, remove all furniture, and redecorate—a few days before Christmas.

If only Leela had owned one of those newsboy caps, some rags to wear, and could put a little soot on her cheeks to look as pathetic as she felt.

The last dish clunked into place in the cupboard. "I guess I'll head home." Emily got her coat. "I guess he's not texting back." The side of her mouth tugged into a smirk.

"I can give you a ride home. It's cold tonight."

"Can I say good night to Uncle Frank before I go?"

Leela's phone chimed.

"It's him!" Emily lit up, and she clutched her fists together at her throat. "Read it."

Leela took a steadying breath and pulled out the text.

He's not icky. I guarantee it.

Again, her fingers flew faster than her good sense. *Guarantee? What kind of guarantee?*

He responded right away. *Look, you can be the judge. If you decide he's "icky," I'll take you to lunch to make up for it.*

Now *that* sounded like a date. Leela almost hoped the new owner would be icky. *Done,* she responded.

Emily did a cheerleader jump beside her, the Herkie one with a bent leg. "You're going out with Jay Wilson! Give me a Jay! Give me a Jay! What's it spell?"

"It spells calm down, Emily. He didn't ask me out." But even Leela had to admit the texts read like flirtations. "Changing the subject. What kind of cookies should I bake for the Cookie House? I'm ruining a whole lot of flour doing research."

"That's so easy it's ridiculous." Emily flicked a stray crumb off the countertop. "I don't know why you're wasting time on that garbage when you should be making Aunt Freesia's gingersnap cookies. Hello. She baked them every year for the Cookie House. Everyone will be expecting you to bring them, especially if you're running the event. Which you will be, right?"

No kidding. But it wasn't that easy. "Except I can't—because I can't find the recipe anywhere. And I'm apparently not great at winging it." Five failed attempts at reverse engineering them proved it. "I have to come up with something else."

"Yeah, that or you could drive me home, come inside, and just get the recipe back from my mom. She raided Aunt Freesia's recipe box a few years ago. Aunt Freeze let Mom take the ginger cookies card since she had it memorized."

No way. It had been at Emily's house all this time?

And gingersnaps are Jay Wilson's favorite.

Jay hadn't outright agreed to show up tomorrow morning, but if he did, Leela had a plan to sweeten her case for the Layton Mansion as Cookie House, literally.

Chapter 6

Jay

"Yeah, I am still interested in the buy-in." Jay paced on the front porch of the Layton Mansion, talking to Rance the brokering agent for the vet clinic's partnership, who loved an early-morning phone call. Snow fell in clusters of flakes so heavy they bent the leaves on the chinaberry bushes beside the veranda. "I'll be procuring the funds in a few days."

"You do hear the clock ticking, though." Rance sounded stern for pre-dawn negotiations, like he hadn't gotten his morning caffeine yet.

"I hear it. And I really appreciate Precious Companion holding it for me. I had the results of my boards forwarded to them today. I assume they received them?"

"Yes. Great scores, young man, which is why they are anxious to move forward."

"Trust me, I'm as anxious as they are."

"Yes, but can you give my clients any reassurance? I'm getting a lot of possibly empty promises. How will you be getting the funds, Dr. Wilson?"

Dr. Wilson—wow. That sounded strange. But he could get used to it. "My real estate agent assures me that my house sale is almost a sure thing."

"Almost and sure thing don't go together well."

Time to feign total confidence. "I will have them for you by New Year's Eve, as discussed. Is there some other problem, Rance?" Pushing back sometimes helped negotiations, right?

"Precious Companion has had another offer, for cash."

"My offer will be cash." Probably.

"This offer is ready now, funds in hand. Doctors Foster and Cody will honor their agreement with you, since that's the kind of businessmen they are. But with another offer on the table—willing to put down money sooner"—Rance did his best hard-sale money-grubber impression—"if you want to guarantee your position, I suggest you move up the timeline."

They couldn't do that to him. New Year's would already push it. "Move it up to when?"

. "The third Tuesday in December."

That was mere days away! Was it even possible to finish the attic, list the house, and get the sale money deposited in that amount of time?

Well, it would have to be. *I need this job.*

"I'll have it."

His phone burned in his hand. To blazes with the attic project—Jay was selling now, with all the contents included.

He pressed the screen to dial Burt Basingstoke. Jingo Layton couldn't put fifty million contingencies of sale in his will. There had to be a way around it.

A car pulled up in front of the house. Leela. He stuck his phone in his pocket.

Maybe one day cleaning out the attic wouldn't hurt.

"Hey, there." Up she walked to where he stood on the wraparound porch. In the morning sun, her eyes were even more sparkling than yesterday.

"Hey. You look nice today." Really nice. A red turtleneck sweater poked out from beneath her coat's collar. It set off her skin, making it rosy. "That sweater's nice."

She looked like she didn't know how to take the compliment. "I didn't know for sure if you'd show up. You were kind of cagey in your text."

"Cagey?" He'd meant to be direct. Well, other than not telling her point blank that he owned the place. Last night, over texting, he should have told her straight out, but then she'd accused him of being—what was her word?—icky. "How is your father?"

"He's all right. Thanks. Just a fall."

"That doesn't sound good." It sounded scary.

"Emily helped him. He's always better after a drink of grape soda." She seemed to be taking it in stride, like this was just par for the course. "I brought you something." In the dim of the pre-dawn morning, a circular sheet of aluminum foil glinted in her hands.

"What's this?"

"It's a bribe."

"I like bribes. Come inside." He stomped his boots on the stoop before entering the big, hollow room. Every footstep on the newly finished wood floors echoed from the basement to the attic. The house, though beautiful, was too empty. "It's arctic this morning."

"If the new owner comes—"

"About the new owner ..." Jay really had to tell her now, but she placed the plate in his hands, distracting him.

"If he comes, I didn't bring him any cookies, so either hide them or else you'll have to share. That's the rule."

"Rule, huh?" He peeked under the foil. "Cookies?" The aroma of ginger, molasses, and cloves floated through his head. "You made gingersnaps?"

"Well, they're soft. They don't exactly *snap*. It's my mom's recipe."

He peeled back the foil and saw a dozen, perfectly round, sugar-crystal-coated cookies in a rich, honey brown.

"You made these?" He lifted one and took a bite. "Jolly holidays!" Jingle bells chimed, Santa chuckled *ho, ho, ho,* and brightly wrapped presents collected under his inner Christmas tree. "These are good."

Understatement.

"To be honest, I tasted them, but I can't trust myself." She slid her shoes off and placed them on the grate. Her socks sported red and white candy-cane stripes. "Are they all right?"

All right? They were a time machine. "My grandma used to make gingerbread cookies, but these are"—his mouth exploded with spices, the taste transporting him back to his childhood—"they're so much better."

Leela stopped her sock-slide across the polished floors. "You're kidding."

"I'm not the type to give empty compliments." He shoved the rest in his mouth and spoke through the chewy goodness. "Seriously incredible."

"I can't believe it." She started to laugh. She covered her mouth with the back of her hand. A tear squeezed out of the laughter-squinted edge of her eye. "For weeks I have made nothing but prize winners for World's Most Disgusting Baked Goods."

"I don't believe it." Nobody who could make cookies like these could fail anything else.

"Trust me. The flour and butter I've tossed in the bin could feed a family of four in a developing nation for a month."

"Are these gingersnaps going to be for sale at the Cookie House thing?" He ate another one.

"They are now."

"Good." He ate two more, barely stopping to chew. He needed trays and trays of these, in succession. "Because I need an infinite conveyor belt of them." *With me at the belt's end with an open mouth,* he thought as he gestured toward the stairwell.

"We're already going upstairs?" They reached the landing, where the second story of the house opened up. "Aren't we going to wait for the owner? Oh, my gosh!" she interrupted herself. "Do you see all these built-ins? The shelves! My friend! Look at all of the readily available places we could stack plates and plates of cookies."

Jay knew all about the built-ins. He'd sanded, primed, and painted every crevice of them. "They don't build details like this into houses anymore."

"No, they don't. Man, and I thought I was in love before, when I'd only seen the outside and the downstairs." She ran her fingertips across the bookcases near the landing, and then went to admire the corner shelves, after which she threw wide some cupboard doors. "Shelf after beautiful shelf! This house was *born* to be the Cookie House." She turned to him. "Where's the owner? Is he already upstairs? Is he meeting us in the attic?"

Wide crevasses between truth and time cracked open. "I meant to tell you yesterday." He turned and led her to the next staircase. It was easier to say this on the move. "I'm afraid you jumped to conclusions."

"Oh, I'm the queen of that. I shouldn't have called the owner icky. Please tell me he doesn't know about that word."

Oh, he knew all right. And after he quit laughing himself into a coughing fit, he'd responded to her text with his guarantee—and the guilty hope that he'd get a date with her. Even if he were leaving for Reedsville soon, he could still go on at least one date with this bright-eyed girl.

They reached the third floor, and across the small first room lay the closed door to the attic. Jay crossed to it and pushed his shoulder against its resistance.

"The owner didn't mind your *icky* word." He pulled the chain on the light fixture, which was a bare bulb. "I mean, I didn't mind." While he climbed the steps, she stayed down by the door.

"I don't follow," she said from below, her hand gripping hard the railing.

He beckoned to her. "No, seriously, it's safe. The structure of the stairs is as sound as the rest of the house."

"No, I mean I don't follow what you're saying." She took only a single step upward but stopped again. "You did or you didn't tell the owner about my gauche comment?"

"You told him." He pushed open the door at the top of the narrow staircase, and it swung to reveal the attic. Oh, merciful roast goose dinners, what a sight! Boxes stacked floor to ceiling from wall to wall, like Tetris, but a whole lot dustier. "Whoa."

Leela appeared at his side, huffing. "What do you mean, *I* told him? I don't even know who—whoa." She looked around, the two of them standing paralyzed side by side. A joint overwhelm petrified them both. Human limestone.

"It's a lot."

"Whoa," Leela breathed again. "What is all this stuff?"

"It's the home improvement task." Somehow the word Herculean needed to fit into that phrase. "All of it has to go before the house can go up for sale."

Leela chortled. "You're telling me the owner expects me to clean this out?"

"Not all by yourself."

"Still! Speaking of guarantees, Jay Wilson, this here chore had better be in exchange for a guarantee of using the Layton Mansion not only this year's but every third Tuesday in December forevermore. It'll have to be grandfathered into every future sales contract."

Wait. *What?* Jay's knee buckled. "Did you say the third Tuesday in December?"

"Yeah." She swept aside a curtain of cobwebs. "I told you yesterday. The Cookie House is always held on the third Tuesday in December."

He raced through his memory banks but couldn't locate that conversation. "That's not a great day for it. Can it be changed?"

"Are you kidding?" She whistled the tune from that *Fiddler on the Roof* "Tradition" song. "Massey Falls' whole lifeblood revolves around it. School is canceled. No sporting events or concerts are scheduled for that night. The local churches all clear their calendars, too. Third Tuesday in December is written in stone as the Christmas Cookie House fundraiser and the Holiday Ball."

No budging. Was it his mind, or had all the boxes just cloned themselves? "It's a big deal. I see that."

"Huge. Bigger than pasta is to Italy." Leela stepped closer to him, her eyes alight with energy—energy from how important this obviously was to her. Not just the town. Her gaze penetrated him to the glowing center. "And you, Jay, can make this year's event happen. Convince the owner for me."

"I'm the owner." There, he'd said it.

But Leela hadn't heard him. "Do this, and you'll embrace the culture of the community, save the Cookie House. Everyone will love you and bring their business to you."

"Business?" He hadn't told her about Precious Companion. Or the fact he was a veterinarian.

"You know. As a Massey Falls real estate agent. You're working with my cousin-in-law, right? Burt?"

"Uh, yes, and no." That's what she'd thought he was all this time? His mind raced back through all their conversations. Yeah, he could see how she might have gathered that—and also why he hadn't caught on until now. "He's working with me, more like."

"Don't get ahead of yourself. Burt's been in business here a long time."

"No, I mean I'm not a real estate agent."

"You're … not?" The sides of her mouth tensed. "Then why did you bring me up in this attic?" True fear clouded her face, like she was waiting for him to reveal he was one of those handsome psychopaths. "Please, dude. I told everyone I was coming here. I posted it on social media. I sent texts to my cousins and their husbands, one of whom is on Massey Falls City Council. You're not going to get away with it."

Whoa, whoa, whoa. "Hey, Leela." She was cute when she was terrified. Ooh, that sounded like a psycho killer thing to think. "I'm not a killer. I'm not a real estate agent. I'm a veterinarian and"—he said it louder this time, so she couldn't mistake his words—"I'm the owner of the Layton Mansion."

Chapter 7

Leela

"The owner!" Leela took a step backward, bumping into a tower of dusty boxes, toppling it sideways into another stack. "Oh!" She whirled around and threw out her arms to steady it. She righted a few box stacks. Once they were secured, she turned back to Jay, her feelings jamming up and straining her speech. "You … deceived me."

"I meant to tell you several times. Honest, I tried to tell you."

"Not hard enough." How embarrassing! Lame comments had flowed like … something really lame. The stairs beckoned, *Leave now, before you embarrass yourself even more.* "You let me go on and on about *the owner.* And it was you."

"The second I realized you'd confused me with a real estate agent, I came clean. I did try before that."

Seriously? Well, he had said something last night—*I need to clarify something*—right when Emily had called about Dad. Okay, so maybe he *had* tried, and she'd cut him off. So this was partly her fault.

"You do know what this makes you, Jay Wilson?" Her mind pounced on a sole word, and she uttered it: *"Icky."*

Jay blinked a few times at her. "I guess you're right." Something about the way he bit both his lips told her he was biting back laughter.

"Yes, I'm right." Of course she was. Any guy who let a girl talk to him like he was a real estate agent and not the owner of the property was totally icky. Well, at least pesky. Icky had different connotations. Still ... come on.

"You know what this means, don't you?" he said. "That as the officially-designated-*icky* owner of the Layton Mansion, I am bound by honor to take you to lunch. Where's good?"

She let her hands slide off her hips and tucked them into her jacket pockets. "Robintino's has good ravioli." Her pasta and Italy metaphor from a minute ago, hard at work.

"I love Italian." He stepped toward her, his hands outstretched. "Will you forgive me?"

She slid her hands from her jacket pockets and accepted his. The touch rippled up her hands, arms, shoulders—not the zapping electricity of yesterday, threatening wildfire. Instead, it was a soft rain, dousing her embers of anger.

"I forgive you." It was a misunderstanding more than a deception, right?

"Thanks. Robintino's it is, then."

Pasta and forgiveness went very well together. When had a man ever before apologized to her? Uh, never? Come to think of it, up until now, every guy who'd wronged her had instantly denied responsibility for it.

Side-eyes at you, Blaine. Wherever you are.

"But there'd better be dessert." Because he seriously could have tried harder.

"What's a meal without dessert?"

"I like the way you think." Their eyes met, and for the first time in a long time, Leela was speaking the same language as a man. Plus, he had warm hands on this cold day. "If we have a whole attic to sort, we'd better get started."

"Seriously?" Jay turned to look at the massive mess looming all around them, and then back at Leela with surprise. "You're staying? To help me?"

"I told you I'd help and I will." She shrugged out of her jacket and threw it aside, tugging at the hem of her slightly-too-snug sweater. "Besides, I still need this place for the Cookie House—and you did agree to persuade the owner."

Jay gave her a once-over. It made her blush.

"I think you're the one accomplishing the persuasion." His eye, like tinsel, glinted on her inner Christmas tree. Sun sparkled on the icicles of her soul. Months here in Massey Falls, and not one flicker of anything with anyone. Now, in less than a day, Jay Wilson had ignited some serious sparks of interest. *If I'm not careful, he'll be pouring kerosene all over my dried up forest and blasting it with a flame thrower.* Which was what came from being in such a long relationship drought.

"So, the deal is I help with the attic, and we get this house ready for you to list—but you agree to let me host the Cookie House here on the third Tuesday in December?"

He reached into his pocket and handed her a box-cutting knife, then looked with obvious dismay at the stacks. "I'm not sure we can be done by the *fifteenth* Tuesday in December, let alone the third Tuesday in December." He looked around with a doubtful smirk. "I can't believe the floor doesn't collapse under the weight of all these boxes."

Leela accepted the knife from him, but truth sliced her: Jay Wilson was here to *sell* a house, not to settle in Massey Falls.

She'd heard that not knowing history left a generation doomed to repeat it.

Then why, when she actually *did* know her own dating history, was she seemingly stuck on an instant replay loop?

Dust swirled. She might as well slash open the boxes. "Let's get this deal done."

Chapter 8

Jay

One by one, Jay pulled box after box from the stack. He would open it and describe its contents. Acting as scribe, Leela would record what was in each box. Then Jay used a sharpie marker and numbered the box.

Three or four boxes into the project, they were in a groove. Small talk could finally erupt into the dusty air. Leela kicked it off.

"If you're not in real estate, what do you do, Jay?"

"I'm a vet."

"Which kind? Animal or military?"

"Ha. I guess that's a valid question. Veterinarian. I finished school this spring. Took my boards and am ready to start practicing." Jay was all about being clear with her from here on out. Even though he hadn't *technically* told her a hundred percent yes on the date for her event.

I'll think of some way to make it work.

"And for graduation you bought yourself a house on Society Row in a charming small town?"

"I inherited this place from Jingo Layton, my uncle. It surprised me, since we weren't close. I'd never even been to Massey Falls before this summer."

"And now you're going to be a vet in Massey Falls. Wow." She sliced open the tape that secured it, and Jay slid off the lid.

"Congratulations, Dr. Wilson."

Not exactly, but before he could clarify, she asked him, "Are you a dog or a cat person?"

"Both. Dogs more, but still cats." A ghost-of-Yellow-Labrador-Retrievers-yet-to-come had played in the house beside Jay while he refinished the wainscoting. "You?"

"Both."

Good answer.

"Plus bunnies," she said, peeking inside the box. "I had a house rabbit when I was a kid."

"Seriously?"

"Yep. It was litter box-trained and everything. Bun-Bun. She was so cute, hopping around the house, hiding under the sofa." She smiled, and it took up her whole face. Man, Leela had a great smile. "As a vet would you have to treat people's pet reptiles?"

"Yeah, part of the job." Not the part he would relish, but … Suddenly, he was telling Leela things. Real things. "To tell the truth, though, I'm more interested in large animals. Horses, cows. Their anatomy is the most fascinating to me. But I'll have to put that on hold, since the clinic I'm going to work in is more house-pet oriented."

"There's a small animal clinic in Massey Falls? I thought Dr. Harrison was strictly a large-animal vet." Leela lifted some items from the box she was sorting, but set them back down and turned to Jay. "Massey Falls is great business for a large animal veterinarian. Practically everyone in town has a hobby farm. More horses per capita than any other incorporated city in the state, and even a few places that raise thoroughbreds."

"Is that right?" How had he not known that? Examining and doctoring for thoroughbreds had been a dream of his, especially for racing thoroughbreds. "Any stables I might have heard of?"

"Whitmore Thoroughbreds is probably the most prominent one right now."

Jay had heard of Whitmore. "Didn't they own a winner of the

Torrey Stakes last year?"

"Yeah. Rose Red is quite a personality-filled mare, I hear. They tout her even more, since their other stakes-winning horse, Snow White, had to be put down this summer. Hey, my cousin Pippa is married to his son. I could introduce you to Dr. Harrison, if you like."

Jay would have liked that very much—if he weren't already entrenched in the deal with Precious Companion. "Actually, my plan is to join a small animal practice over in Reedsville." His big plans felt smaller, somehow, than thoroughbreds all of a sudden. "If things work out."

And if they did, on his timeline, he'd be messing up her world. Jay's stomach clenched. *But I'm only a jerk if Burt really does have a buyer.* Did Burt have one?

"Then you'll head to Reedsville." Her voice sounded a little dead. Why? He shouldn't flatter himself that she was disappointed at the idea he might go. They'd only just met. How could she care? She didn't, obviously. Not about him.

Oh. The house. Right. Not him.

Jay squirmed as he took down another box and sliced open the crumbling tape on top.

An idea hit him. If he could get Burt to write it into the sales contract that she could use the mansion on that day, and then the new owners could take possession—that would solve it, right? Any new owner wouldn't let a little delay sink a deal, right? Especially anyone with the Christmas spirit in their hearts or who loved Massey Falls like they should—according to Leela's standard of appreciating fundraisers and service organizations.

The new buyer could sign, transfer the money to Jay, and wait to move in until after Leela's cookie event. Right?

Totally possible. Everyone in the world was altruistic and community-minded. It would be no problem.

A little puff of dust went up his nose, or maybe it itched because he was lying to himself. "So, I did mention we're cleaning this out so I can list the house for sale, right?"

"You did." She looked around at the cobwebs, wrapping a nearby big fluffy one around her hand like her fingers were a paper cone and the spiders had made gray cotton candy. "If I owned it, I probably couldn't let it go. It's not just beautiful, it's too sentimental."

"Cobwebs are sentimental?"

She shot him a look that let him know his joke was lame. "Don't you have any feeling toward it? Think of all the work you've put in."

"It's hard to be sentimental about a place I'd never seen before I inherited it." The mansion represented a *means* to an end, not a place to end up. "And that extends to the attic. In fact, I'll be shocked if there's anything I'll consider sentimental up here."

"Really? Nothing connected to your family's past calls to you from up here?"

"You mean like this macramé owl"—he tugged it from the box— "or this ceramic bullfrog with a dish scrubber in its mouth?" None of it called to him even in the faintest voice from the deepest well.

"Fine. I'll give you that. But then why do the big clean-out?"

"It's part of the will that I need to clean it out before I can sell it, but it probably needs a de-junking no matter what. The place is a fire hazard."

"Well, I'm holding out hope that we find something really valuable."

If by valuable she meant sentimental, Jay would be shocked if there was even one box with a single item with so-called value. And if by valuable, she meant an item that could be sold at an auction—or even a junky yard sale—for more than fifty cents, he'd be just as shocked.

"Although, I'll admit," she said, "according to the inventory list so far, things aren't looking that way."

At least her sentimentality wasn't making her delusional.

They slogged through boxes and floated through conversations all morning long. First childhood pet stories, then college roommate nightmares, and most-embarrassing-moments tales. Leela crushed him with those. He went into a coughing fit, laughing so hard about her temporary plastic yellow tooth on the night of the prom.

This girl was funny. And totally easy to talk to. It'd been a long time since Jay had spent more than a few minutes talking with any girl.

Too long.

"Are you worried about anything?" He held up a fountain pen with a quill and she scrawled the additional item on her inventory list. "Going into vet practice, I mean."

The question pried open a sealed envelope inside him. He examined the contents. Yeah. Really worried. "Probably that someone's beloved pet will die based on a mistake I make."

"Everything dies." She paused and got quieter. "Everyone dies."

Leela's mom's loss tingled in the room.

"I bet you miss your mom."

"Every minute. Like oxygen, or the color blue." Leela set down her pencil and notebook for a thoughtful second, but she took them up again just as quickly. "That was her cookie recipe, the gingersnaps. So, I guess in a way that means now you know a tiny bit about her."

A woman's perfect recipe was definitely an insight into a soul. "I like everything about your mom that I know so far." A sudden need to inquire seized him. "Tell me more about her."

Late-morning light streamed in through the dormer and onto Leela's face, glancing across her eyes and making them a brighter blue than ever.

"My mom was classy." Leela looked like she had floated somewhere far away. "Oh, she might not have lived on Society Row, but she taught the women who lived there a lot. Like, that being refined included being kind, not gossipy. That it required inclusion, not exclusion. That the highest pursuit is the betterment of mankind, not the betterment of your hairstyle or your bank account or your landscaping."

"Good lessons for anyone."

"My mom raised all the sights and standards and ambitions of all

51

the women in town—to make Massey Falls the best it could be. The Cookie House was her brainchild, actually."

Oh. A thunderbolt struck Jay's chest. No wonder this thing was important to Leela.

"Then, when Dad had his accident, she had to more or less withdraw from public life to care for him—and that was an example and lesson to them as well, in choosing priorities. She was the best mom, and the best person I could have imagined."

It sounded like it. Jay's mom was good, too, but in a very different way. Life had been unkind to her, but she'd survived it the best way she knew how.

"And her gingersnaps taste like Christmas on a plate."

This brought a smile. "I'll teach you to make them—if you like."

He pictured Leela Miller in an apron, a dusting of flour on her nose. "Definitely." Unbidden, he then pictured taking the curvaceous, red-sweater-clad beauty in his arms, looking into those impossibly bright eyes, lightly kissing away that dusting of flour ... "Soon."

"Good." Leela exhaled and smiled at him, her eyes happy again. "Let's get back to work."

Right. To work. So that this attic could be finished and Jay could call Burt and list the house, and ... betray Leela.

"Maybe we should grab lunch. And possibly dinner." His *icky factor* had just moved to the two-meal requirement.

"One last box, and then we go." Leela pulled one off the latest stack. "What's this?"

Inside it lay something Jay never expected to see when he'd agreed to clean out the attic.

Chapter 9

Leela

Inside this final box of the morning were some teenage girl items—dried roses, a photo album, two diaries, a pile of pictures, several folded notes. "Whose are these?" She tugged out the quilted photo album and opened the quilted cover. "Someone put a lot of love into making this."

Finally, something that wasn't worthless kitsch!

"Probably someone we don't know." Jay put the albums aside and dug a little more in the box. "We can toss the flowers, at least."

What did he mean, at least? "But not the photo album or diary!" Leela lifted the photo album's puffy, fabric-lined cover. "Oh, look. They're so cute. Look at their hair." Hairstyles from thirty years ago fluffed out, filling the school photos to their very edges. "It's such a good thing you didn't just throw this in the trash. It's got to belong to someone."

"That's the problem. All of this stuff is valuable to *someone,* but I have no idea how to figure out who the someones are. No other heirs are coming out of the woodwork to claim things, even though the lawyers have contacted them repeatedly."

Hard to believe. "Not even your mom?" Jay's mom was Jingo's sister, wasn't she?

"Especially not my mom."

"Have you asked her?"

"Let's just say when I brought it up, she said she would rather chew rusty nails than come back here."

"That's strong language."

"Not as strong as the other things I won't repeat."

Interesting. And sad. "Why's she so hostile?" How terrible that she hated this place that much. A place so beautiful! What had happened to turn her against it?

"It's a long story."

Probably. But maybe, if Jay could only decide to keep the place instead of selling it and moving to Reedsville, his mother would have a chance to come back and make amends with her past. But that didn't seem likely, considering the way he talked, and his urgency at finishing the attic clean-out.

"Can I take a look at that?" Jay reached for the album. "That's— my *mom*." He sat down and peered at it.

Leela slid over to sit beside where he held the book in the shaft of winter sunlight coming through the dormer window. "She's so darling."

"Look at this." He pointed to a picture, leaning in so Leela's shoulder touched his, and his hip was flush with hers.

Man, he smelled good. Mingled with the dust, his manly scent interrupted her concentration. Until she really saw the photograph, that is.

Dark eyes stared out at them, solemn, contemplative. They were Jay's eyes, minus the jaunty twinkle. What a beautiful, sober child. "How old was she here?"

"I don't know. Nine, maybe?" He lifted page after page. His mom grew older with each turn. "There's Uncle Jingo. He was decades older than Mom. From Grandpa Layton's first wife."

"Who's that?" A second young girl grinned beside Jay's mom, now maybe twelve. On this sole page, a non-photo was inserted—a handwritten note in pink pen and young girl handwriting. "Hereby let it be known that I, Ceri Layton—"

54

"It's pronounced *Keri*."

"Oh. Right. I, Ceri Layton, shall grow up to have a son."

A new handwriting took over. "And I, shall grow up to have a daughter."

The first handwriting resumed with, "And they will grow up and fall in love and get married. Then we can be sisters!" The *we* sported a triple underline.

Leela's eyes fell on the signatures: Ceri Layton, and Freesia Youngblood.

"Mom?" Leela gasped. She tugged the photo album to her own lap and touched the photo's edge with her fingertip.

"Freesia Youngblood is your mom?" Jay looked at the picture, at Leela, and then back at the picture. "You look like her. Same cute dimple. She was my mom's best friend."

Leela ran a finger over her mom's juvenile handwriting, the looping *l*, the *i* dotted with an open circle. "I miss her."

When she came up to this attic, she'd never expected to find her mother.

What a sweet, tender mercy. It was like Mom was here in this moment, smiling, her dimple deep, her pain gone, and ready to listen to everything Leela had been feeling over the past few months without her. Like Leela could almost reach out and hug her.

Jay put an arm around Leela's shoulders—almost like he'd been bidden to do so. A wash of warmth filled Leela's every cell.

"Thanks for letting me be here, Jay," she whispered.

Jay slid closer, his breath sharing her own, and he looked at the picture of their moms. "It's good to see my mom looking so happy." He ran his finger lightly over the words on the page, just like Leela had. "Really good."

Without thinking, Leela tipped her head onto Jay's shoulder. It was a perfect fit. The air around them tingled like Christmas morning's goodness, and she reveled in the feeling that both Mom and love were not far away.

Leela closed her eyes and just breathed it all in. Jay let her. It was as if he felt what she was feeling.

Jay's fingers slid closer to hers on the photo album page, and his pinky entwined with hers, making little lights twinkle inside her mind, and making everything else tingle.

He pressed his other hand flat against the cellophane covering the photo and the diary page. "I didn't expect to find *this* in an attic."

"This connection to your family?" she asked, a little breathless.

"Or to you."

Sugar rushed through her veins, and she hadn't even tasted the gingersnaps this morning.

Did he really have to move to Reedsville? Just when she was getting to know him? There was more to explore—especially this history between their moms. Wasn't there? He saw it too, right?

Chapter 10

Jay

Leela's stomach growled, breaking the spell that had settled over them.

"Lunch?" he asked lamely, breaking their silence, and signaling the end of whatever that freaky-amazing thing was they'd shared. "I hear from a reliable source that Robintino's has great ravioli." Jay helped her to her feet, and they headed for the stairs.

He had never been woven into such magic with a woman before. What did it mean that he was fascinated and terrified of the almost molecular bonding he'd felt with Leela for those brief—and seemingly eternal—moments?

"You're calling me reliable?"

Wholly. And all the other good adjectives swirled around her, too. He tugged the door at the top of the stairs closed behind them. The frame must have swollen from years of disuse.

"It's a much bigger job than I originally expected when Burt told me about it. I pictured a day, tops."

"I hate to say so, but it looks more like six months."

Six months with Leela in the attic every day could turn into something off the charts, if they had another repeat of this morning.

"Six months or a big, metal trash roll-off and a torch." He locked up the house behind him and led her to his car.

"Except for that photo album." She settled into the passenger side, and he went around and started the car.

"No, I'll be keeping a tight hold on that." *Mom might actually like to see it.*

At Robintino's, they both ordered ravioli. The plates arrived, steaming with a creamy tomato sauce, but Leela didn't pick up her fork.

"About that photo album and diary," she said. "It's funny isn't it? Seems like someone had plans for us."

That was funny, but not in a ha-ha sense. More like an uncanny funny. "Before we were even born."

Leela lifted her blue eyes from her plate, and her gaze seared him to the center. "Before they knew how well we'd get along."

Jay swallowed hard. "We do get along. Don't we." It wasn't a question. It was a declaration—mostly to himself.

The ravioli steamed between them. Beneath the table, his ankle brushed hers.

Something was happening here. Something different. And—he didn't want to relinquish his man card, but he had to admit—a little scary. Like his life might be taking a wild turn.

No. I have it all laid out. Reedsville. Cats and dogs. The partnership.

"Have I told you how I got a giant, t-shaped scar on my knee?" he asked, and the steam cleared.

Leela blinked. "*You* have a t-shaped knee scar, too?"

Conversation flowed like the sauce on their plates, mellow and savory. For two hours, they filled the air with stories, from the time the retiree customer in her bookshop proposed out of the blue to the time he nearly got his cornea scratched by a fierce cat during a clinical. "Had to wear an eye-patch for two weeks. I looked like that guy on *Agents of Shield.*"

"At least it gave you an excuse to talk like a pirate. My dad used to say *shiver me timbers* all the time. Since he was a tree surgeon, he said he had a right to use the phrase."

"He sounds cool." And like someone she loved very much. "Can I ask what happened to him?"

"If you really want to know."

He did.

"He loved his job. Then one fateful day that changed everything. The trunk that fell on him was so heavy. Almost a full ton, they said. A crushed spine is tough to recover from. A crushed spinal cord even harder."

"Wow." Nothing Jay could think to say felt adequate. "You say he *used* to talk like a pirate. Now …?"

"The accident took his speech along with it."

Clearly, she missed her dad, too. The dad she'd known. "How old were you?"

"Fifteen. Nine years ago." She talked about the things he *could* do. "He struggles, but he has a fighting spirit. We do exercises every day. He can drink grape soda through a straw really well. And he can feed himself most of the time now, especially when we get Mexican food from El Toro. Life's getting better. Slowly. I'm learning things, and so is he."

What an incredible way to view such a hardship. Leela Miller was much more than a gorgeous blue-eyed woman with a great smile and an obsession with community service, whose figure looked like Marilyn Monroe's in a turtleneck sweater.

Around Leela, Jay didn't want to just be a veterinarian. He wanted to be some kind of hero, someone she could describe in the way she described her dad—with admiration and wonder.

I want to be a hero when I'm with her.

"You've never mentioned your dad." Leela pushed a crust of garlic bread around on her plate. "Is it okay if I ask why?"

"He wasn't around much. I barely remember him. My mom went through some stuff when she was younger. She claimed she was hard to get along with, and that she pushed him away." Yeah, there was more to that story, but no sense dragging Mom's reputation through the mud with Leela—even though it was all so unfair.

"Dads shouldn't leave."

"No. I know that. Which is why I've sworn I'll never leave a child. Or a wife, for that matter. When I was a kid, I put a lot of blame on my dad for leaving; now I can see she played a part, but it doesn't excuse him entirely."

"Yeah." Leela reached across the table and placed a soft hand on his arm. Some of the thorns that were always there inside him seemed to slide out of his soul. Jay hadn't ever really talked about this with anyone, let alone with a woman on a first date.

Is this a date?

"Where is she now?"

"Torrey Junction." Not close, but not that far, either.

"Could you invite her over? To see your work on the house?"

"Like I say, she won't come." She'd been pretty clear about her feelings on the mansion and the town.

The meal ended, but the conversation didn't, and they drove through a snowstorm back to the Layton Mansion, which looked more and more like a Dickens fantasy as the snow ensconced it.

Was he going to miss that sight when he uprooted and moved to Reedsville?

Or, the bigger question: was he going to miss Leela Miller's company and conversation?

Uh, maybe there'd be someone just like her in Reedsville.

He sneezed. Pinocchio's nose grew; Jay's sneezed.

Chapter 11

Leela

Lunch had run long. Leela should go home, but Jay Wilson was a supermagnet to her soul. She couldn't seem to pry herself away from his overwhelming pull.

She texted Aunt Sal. *Can you keep Dad for the afternoon?*

Emily said you're on a date. Take all the time you need. Well, until dinner. I have to go brew up the witching hour as soon as all my kids get home.

"You need help this afternoon?" she asked. "Turns out I have some time."

Back in the attic, they carefully set aside the photo album and the diary, and then they got to work digging through the next stack.

"A stack an hour is about our progress rate, I'm calculating," she said, inventory ledger at the ready.

"I love your optimism."

Love? Her heart did a little flippity-do-dah—until she tamped it down. Figure of speech. Not a declaration.

Idiot. It wasn't like Jay had felt the scary-strong bonding Leela had while they were in the enchantment of seeing the diary.

Unless he had. How could he not? And then there had been that moment over lunch as the steam of the ravioli rose between them. At least it hadn't whispered again.

Was she losing it?

No. Because next he started asking about her dating life. *Bless him. And curse him at the same time.* He was leaving town, for Pete's sake. She should not get on this amusement park ride.

"So, Massey Falls is pretty small, eh?" he said. "What's the single life like?"

"Do you seriously need to ask that?" Leela tucked her box knife in her pocket. "It's somewhere between a social desert and the planet Mars."

He made a grunting sound. "Reedsville is probably better, I guess."

Stab-stab-stab! What made him say that? "Chuh," she grunted.

"What's *chuh* for?" He set down the wooden bowl of glass grapes he'd just unwrapped from old newspaper. "Are you all right?"

Her face must be showing her disgust. "I—let's just say I don't want to date in Reedsville." She quickly scribbled *glass grapes* onto her inventory list.

"You can't just throw something like that out there and not elaborate."

It'd been so long since Blaine, but it still stung like swimming with angry jellyfish. Maybe talking about it with someone would help. She hadn't even told Mom. "There was a guy. I dropped out of college and followed him to Reedsville." Yep, dropped out, gave up her education, everything. For Blaine. "We dated. I worked in the bookstore. Things were going well."

"And?"

"And he was offered a promotion down the coast." At which point, Blaine hadn't offered Leela a ring. "He took it."

"But he didn't take you along." Jay slowly turned his head from side to side. Under his breath, he muttered, "Idiot."

Idiot. It re-echoed. Yeah. Blaine *was* an idiot. Leela was a catch! A devoted, bright girlfriend who'd sacrificed for him. And he left her for … what?

Idiot. Yeah.

With a single word, Jay had shooed away thousands of stinging jellyfish accumulating for years on Leela's soul.

A deep breath. Nope, they were still gone. *Miracle. The idiot miracle.* There was something about this attic. Something enchanted.

Okay, maybe it's not the attic. Maybe it's Jay Wilson.

Ugh! But he was leaving. Going to Reedsville. And for all the reasons in the world, Leela was not going back there.

Besides, a guy with smoldering good looks like him had to have a relationship burning somewhere. Mansion Hottie, as Emily called him, would be fighting off women, pelting them with dog food to keep them at bay.

"How about you? Dating someone?"

"Huhhhh," he let out a long sigh. "High school, I was a total geek. Then in college, I was studying to get into vet school, which is harder than you'd think. Barely made it. Then, veterinary school turned me into a monk. Then I moved straight to Massey Falls."

"Enough said." She tried to keep her voice level and not let the shriek of excitement creep in. "I know there's no one to date in this town."

"So you're not dating anyone now?" he asked. How much hope did she detect in his tone? Some? Any? "Besides me, I mean."

"Oh, are we dating?" *Please say yes.* "I thought this was a charity gig."

"That's what I made you think, to get you to go out with me. I'm always using my pity-date card. It works best with kind-hearted women."

Please. "I guess it's just you, then. Since you owe me dinner still." He'd promised. Not like Leela would forget something like that.

"How about tonight?"

"You haven't gotten sick of me yet? We've been together since dawn."

"Sorry. You'll have to try harder to make me sick of you."

"Fine. I have some Laffy Taffy jokes for you. Animal-related, for your veterinarian taste." One about a giraffe poised itself on her tongue, and one about an elephant and a rhino. "Ready?"

"Arrrgh!" He threw his head back as if in pain, laughing at the ceiling, and it bounced around in the rafters of the attic.

"There's the pirate-speak we all knew was lying dormant in you." She pushed his shoulder. He caught her hand and pulled her to him. She relaxed into him. He smelled like attic dust and Robintino's and sawdust.

"So you'll go to dinner with me?"

"I wish I could, but Dad needs me tonight." Aunt Sal had spent all day already.

"Oh." Did he really sound as disappointed as she wanted that sound to be? "Another time, then."

"Maybe the night of the Cookie House. It's also …" She choked back all the fear gathering in her throat. "It's also the Holiday Ball that night. I do need a date for that."

Chapter 12

Jay

The Holiday Ball! What the bloom was that? And it was the same night as this Cookie House thing, and the day his payment was due to Precious Companion? Sure, the idea of seeing Leela Miller dressed in a sexy gown had its appeal—almost as much as the idea of holding her close while music played.

"Sure," he said, ignoring the trouble the calendar hollered at him. "It would be an honor."

She giggled, and that was reason enough not to backtrack. Her laugh was like a little handful of jingle bells.

"Actually, I'd better get home." She checked the time on her phone. She got to her feet, smoothed that ruby-red sweater over her luscious curves, and reached for her jacket. "I'll see you tomorrow."

"Tomorrow?" Wait. She was coming back again? "Don't you have other stuff to do?" Like take care of her dad, or not spend a day in a dusty attic?

"Not if getting this attic cleaned out means my getting to use the Layton Mansion for the Cookie House event." She donned her jacket, covering up all those curves. "So I'll see you in the morning, then?"

"It's a date." *It's a third date.* And Leela Miller seemed like the type of girl who might kiss on the third date, if he was reading her right.

***

The next morning, she arrived just as Jay pulled up at the house. She got out of her car, balancing two tall cups and a bag. "I hope you like cocoa."

He loved cocoa, and a girl who thought of it. "I haven't lit the fire. It's going to be cold up there for a while until the chimney heats up."

"That's why I brought the cocoa. Let's get after it." Her enthusiasm was palpable. "Maybe we'll find a velvet painting of Elvis up there today. Or a stack of plastic canvas Kleenex box covers."

"Is someone caring for your dad today?"

"I have a lot of family around. Today Uncle Max is going to spend the day with Dad. They have a big bass fishing show they like to watch, and Uncle Max has the day off to Netflix binge it with him. If it warms up, they'll go shopping for some ice-fishing gear."

Good. Jay could have her attention without guilt. He let her into the house. When he flipped on the light, a warm glow filled the front room, warmer than it had seemed before.

Maybe it was the time of day.

"I'll lay the fire."

"Do you need help? I can haul wood from the pile." She clapped her mittens together. "I saw it out there the day I vandalized the window."

They walked out to the woodpile together, and he loaded her with a few logs, taking a pile of his own. "What were you thinking when that happened?"

"That I was going to spend the afternoon in jail."

"Like I'd press charges."

"I thought you were the real estate agent, remember?"

Oh, yeah. They tramped across the snow together, side by side. The light from the front window made a golden square on the snow beside the wraparound porch.

"It's such an amazing place, Jay. How come your mom won't come back?"

Leela was investing enough in the house. Maybe he could just tell her something about Mom and the past. "When she was a teenager here, someone spread some terrible rumors—untrue—about her, and she vowed never to come back."

"I'm so sorry to hear that." Leela reached for his hand. "That must have been so hard for her to deal with, especially if she was young. It sounds like she had to handle it all on her own with no support."

Pretty much. "Her older brother had some issues of his own. I think Jingo eventually felt bad about that." Which might be why he'd made Jay the sole recipient of the mansion in his will. It could have gone to anyone, even a non-relative, but Uncle Jingo had singled out Jay. "She knows I've been clearing out the house, but I didn't want to say too much about the project."

"You're protecting her."

"Maybe so." Jay turned his hand over, and Leela pressed her fingers in between his and squeezed. "It sounds like we've both lost parents, one way or another."

Yeah.

And I'm walking side by side with the one girl who could understand.

Chapter 13

Leela

Day two in the attic with Jay flew by. He had a million stories for her, and somehow, she ended up telling him a million back.

That night, after working for a couple of hours on Cookie House details, she lay in her bed and stared at the ceiling. Dad's health monitors beeped softly from the other room. He'd probably sleep like a baby, after all the shopping with Uncle Max.

Something whispered from the dimness of her room. *You should let everyone else into his life more. He needs people. And so do you.*

Leela blinked, wishing that the voice had come from Mom. But more likely, it came from her own mind.

"I would. But how can I ask people to do it?" And she didn't really want to share him. "People have responsibilities."

People love him. He makes them happier. You should share him.

Leela turned on her side and looked at the wallpaper, little flower clusters among vines. The same wallpaper as she'd looked at every night as a girl growing up in this house.

It was late, but she texted her cousin Pippa. *What are your plans for tomorrow?*

***

Next morning, Jay texted to tell her he was bringing breakfast and to leave it to him. And he'd buy lunch, too. She'd brought a sack lunch for each of them yesterday. Boring, but time was of the essence, and Robintino's, for all its deliciousness on every level, had eaten up a lot of time.

"I'm expecting a breakthrough today." She walked up the porch, avoiding a snow pile and three icicles. "Three stacks per hour is my prediction." She wanted that for him. He needed to be able to sell it, clearly. It was the least she could do, considering he was making the Cookie House possible. "Maybe four stacks per hour!" She flexed her bicep.

"Cockeyed optimist." He grinned, some morning stubble still on his chin, and offered her a fast food breakfast sandwich. "I hope you like sausage."

"Love it."

Inside, he'd already lit the fire, and they stood near it to eat. "How's your Cookie House stuff going? Do you even have time for it?"

"It's getting there." In fits and starts. Oh, and shoot. How could she forget? "At five, I'm meeting with the Ladies' Auxiliary for a progress report."

"Sounds official."

He had no idea. They were going to want a definite yes on the Layton Mansion, but the attic was still a long way from empty. *I haven't fulfilled my end of the bargain yet.* "We should get to work."

No four-stacks-per-hour progress ensued, but they made a dent. Like someone eating a ten-gallon vat of ice cream with a teeny spoon. They did lunch at a shop that made panini sandwiches that tasted like olive oil and love—but they didn't linger there. They just ate, talked, and got back to the attic.

The sun was setting, and Leela needed to get to the library for the Ladies' Auxiliary meeting soon. *I wish I could just stay here.*

"When are you going to teach me to make those cookies of your mom's?" Jay asked.

"Name the time."

"Tonight?"

Okay. But wasn't he getting tired of her? *I'm not getting tired of him.* No, she was getting almost surgically conjoined. "That will probably work. I have to make sure Dad gets dinner first."

"Who's taking care of him today?"

"My cousin Pippa. Emily's mom offered to help tomorrow, so I'm scheduled to be your attic slave again."

"Is that so?"

Heat rushed through her. "That didn't come out like I intended."

Jay looked at her like he wished the other meaning had been her intent.

"What I mean, is I've got a few days open now. Everyone likes to do service around the holidays."

"Normally I'd say it makes them feel less guilty about so much consumerism, but I suspect they actually love your dad, considering all the stories you've told me about him."

Jay. Jay Wilson. A thousand insights into her life. "If you actually want to make cookies, I'd love the help. I need to make three double batches before I hit the hay tonight or I'll never have enough in the freezer in time for the Cookie House. It's coming right up."

Jay's gaze shot around at the piles, and he definitely looked hopeless for a second. After a moment, he turned back to her. "Let's bake. How's seven?"

"Sounds fine." It sounded dreamy to spend the evening with him, and with nothing to do but wait for the timer to ding on the oven. Maybe they could sit together on the sofa, put their feet up on the coffee table together, and …

Wait. This was her house they were talking about. Her house looked like it had been trashed by a whole raucous gang of naughty-listers. "Hey, so I'll need to check out a little early today." To hire or transform herself into a maid brigade. It was four o'clock already.

"Yeah, Ladies' Auxiliary meeting," he said. "How soon do you need to go?"

Twelve hours ago? *The floor hasn't been vacuumed in a week.*

70

Everyone caring for Dad had been taking him on outings or bringing them to their homes for the day. Dishes piled, and dust had gathered.

"Pretty soon. Or"—she checked her phone's clock, trying to act casual—"now, I guess."

Leela could tell him no, take the pressure off herself.

Okay, no she couldn't. If Jay Wilson wanted to bake with her, why would she resist?

There was one good solution. She sent a text.

Emily! House cleaning SOS!

I'm on my way.

At home, Leela first checked in with Dad, who was still at Pippa's but would be back about six thirty.

The doorbell rang. "Emily! Thanks! We are at DEFCON one. Jay is coming over to bake with me."

Emily stamped in. "Whoa, girl. It looks like a pack of she-wolves has been through here." Emily cringed. "I mean, I know taking care of Uncle Frank is taxing, but, who is making this mess? Not him, surely."

Nope. "All me." She offered a broom. "You sweep, I'll vacuum?"

"On it." Good thing, too. If Jay were to come in and see the house in this state, Mom would swoop back from the Other Side and ream Leela.

Emily cornered Leela in the bathroom by brandishing a mop in one hand and a toilet brush in the other. "So, how are things going with Mansion Hottie Jay?" She held out the vowel in his name. "If he's coming by, there must be something more going on than home improvement."

"We're baking. He said he'd help me since I'm helping him." Not exactly true.

Emily sighed. "He's seriously hot enough to melt all the snow in Massey Falls."

"Does your dad know how boy crazy you are?"

"Hello, pot. My name is kettle."

"I'm not boy crazy."

71

"Seriously? After being within arm's reach of Dr. Jay *all day*? You're barking mad."

Please. "He's selling the house and moving to Reedsville." Leaving. "As soon as we finish the project. I'll probably never see him again."

The bomb left a crater. Emily stared into it. Then, after a minute she said, "Not everybody will leave you, Leela. The right one will stay."

Sure. Whatever. "Let's just finish, okay?"

***

Leela barely had time to shower and dress in something that hadn't been in an attic before rushing to meet with Una Mae, Mrs. Imrich, Mrs. Harrison, and all the other ladies.

In the large conference room of the Massey Falls Public Library, Una Mae called the meeting to order. She wore her festive sweater, the red angora one she told everyone she'd bought in Prague, and pounded her tiny gavel.

"Thank you all for coming to this emergency session to finalize details of the Cookie House and Holiday Ball. Let's keep this short." She shot a wicked glance at Mrs. Harrison, the idle-tangent-talker of the group. "Leela Miller, our chairwoman."

Leela stood. "All the subcommittee chairwomen are on track."

Una Mae cleared her throat like an accusation. "What about the venue?"

Leela's winter boots shrank, pinching her toes. Could she actually report? Sure, she and Jay were moving things along in the Layton Mansion's attic, but the boxes were cloning themselves, and hadn't he said they needed to complete the attic before Leela could use it?

"What is your update, Leela?" Una Mae's eyes tightened at the edges, her frown deepening. "This is the eleventh hour."

It was as if Una Mae didn't know she was the reason for the emergency, by her refusing to let the event happen at her own house as planned.

"Leela Miller. All print fliers and advertising must be finalized. We need to list a location and address. Have you even found a place for the Cookie House? What about the Holiday Ball? Just give us something, please. People are already baking cookies, I believe."

Nods went around the table.

Leela should not be bullied into committing. She hadn't completed her part of the deal with Jay. They were closer, but the attic wasn't done.

Her brain and her mouth were not connected, however.

"I am in negotiations with the new owner of the Layton Mansion to hold both the Cookie House and the Holiday Ball there."

"The Layton Mansion!" Mrs. Harrison blurted, and the two dozen other women hiss-whispered it as well. "Why, that's marvelous, my dear. You are a miracle worker. Everyone will come just to see it. We'll have our best turnout ever! Genius!"

With every phrase of praise from Mrs. Harrison, Una Mae Coldicott's face contorted another degree. Finally, the hubbub died down, and Una Mae harrumphed.

"Well. Yes. But you said you're *in negotiations.* Is nothing set?"

Leela kept her face a stone.

"Miss Miller, you do appreciate the time sensitivity here."

Oh, she did. The ticking of the clock practically deafened her. "I should know very soon." If she asked Jay, he might agree to it, despite the unfinished attic. Right?

I don't know. I don't want to be one of those people who doesn't keep her side of the bargain. Dad would be ashamed. So would Mom, for that matter. It wasn't classy.

"Very soon is not soon enough." The breath went out of the room. All eyes flitted between Leela and Una Mae's showdown. "You either commit, or you remove yourself from the chairwomanship."

But—on the other hand, Mom would have been so proud of her for chairing the event. *I have to show her I can do this.*

"Leela? Can you guarantee the Layton Mansion, or do we cancel the event?"

Gasps rose, and upper lips curled in derision. Mrs. Imrich might have gagged.

Una Mae ignored all the histrionics. "Can you, Leela?"

She couldn't. "I can."

Oh, no. Oh-no-oh-no-oh-no.

"That's done, then." Una Mae Coldicott pounded her gavel, much harder than necessary. It was almost like Leela's promise burned her up. "Mrs. Philbert, print the fliers with the correct address. Mrs. Harrison, contact the radio station to pay for the advertising. Mrs. Young, you'll do our social media blast. Leela?" Una Mae turned a cold eye on her. "You had better not disappoint us. A failure will deplete our coffers, and we won't have a way to replenish, since we'll have to cancel at the last minute and lose all of our investment."

"I'll make sure it happens." Somehow.

Was it possible that the snow was deeper on her walk home? Or did her whole body just sink into it more into it than usual? In her house, she kicked the winter off her boots and shut the door.

This was not ideal.

Before she'd even had a chance to take off her scarf and hat, let alone start making Dad's soup for dinner, Leela's doorbell rang.

Oh, shoot. Jay was here already to make cookies.

Leela had to tell Jay what she'd promised the ladies at Auxiliary. Leela leaned her head against the door for a second. Then she took a deep breath, pasted on a smile and threw the door wide to let Jay in from the cold. "You're early."

"Hey. Yeah. Sorry, but I thought you might not have time to make dinner." Jay stood on the doorstep, a couple of bags in his hands. "I brought take-out. I hope that's okay."

"Come in." She stepped aside for him, and the scent of cumin and garlic wafted in with him.

Well, look at him. He sure cleaned up nicely. In a button-up shirt and dark-wash jeans, he had a whole *off-duty doctor* vibe going on.

She pointed him toward the kitchen, and Leela trailed after him like one of those cartoon mice drawn by the visible, steamy, curling scent of cheese. "Smells amazing. You didn't have to do that."

But bless him for it.

"I hope you like Mexican." He set the bags on the counter.

"Totally." She peeked in a bag. "El Toro?" No way. "El Toro is Dad's favorite."

"I know."

"You do?" How could he? She glanced between the takeout boxes and Jay's face.

"You told me."

"I did?" Oh, right. When he was asking about Mom and Dad. "Thank you for remembering him." Leela's hip hit the countertop, stopping her bowled-overness.

"Plus, no dishes to do." He grinned—almost as if he knew about all the cleaning she'd done today already.

Jay removed the cardstock-covered tinfoil bowls from the bags. "You said he's got mobility issues, but can he eat with us? I brought him enchiladas with beans and rice on the side."

"Of course. Wow. He is so going to love this." Leela set forks and glasses on the table in a flash. "I haven't made him anything spicy in a while."

The door rattled, and Dad came in with help from Pippa, who hugged them both before leaving. Maybe it was the Mexican spices in the air giving him buoyancy, but Dad leaned on Leela's arm a little less than usual.

"Dad, this is Jay Wilson." She helped him to the table. "He inherited the Layton Mansion."

Throughout dinner, Dad didn't really look Jay in the eye or acknowledge him, but he did seem to enjoy the enchiladas. Jay acted like it was no big deal.

Bless him.

Leela wiped Dad's face with the napkin. "We haven't had El Toro since … forever."

Dad groaned something. He blinked a few times.

"What's that, Dad?" Leela leaned to catch his gaze. Their eyes met, and Dad groaned again—something almost intelligible. "I think you said, *Since Freeze left.* Is that right, Dad?" Leela's voice shook as she repeated him. "Because I think you're right. We haven't had it since Mom …"

She couldn't say died. Or passed. Or any of those terrible syllables.

Dad mumbled something else. It sounded a lot like, *I miss my Freeze.*

"I miss her too, Dad." Leela bit her lower lip to kink off the watering hose gushing toward her eyes. "I wish she hadn't needed to leave us."

Jay set his fork down for a moment, watching them almost reverently.

It took a couple of steadying breaths, but Leela composed herself and turned to Jay. "Sometimes it's still pretty raw."

Jay reached over and put a hand on Dad's shoulder. Dad turned to him. Jay gave a curt man-nod. Dad blinked, paused, and then gave one back.

Leela could have kissed Jay right then and there. Communication—with Dad—spurred by a nostalgic meal and genuine kindness.

Brilliant. *Thank you, Jay Wilson.* He might be a healer of more than cats and dogs.

Dinner wrapped up. Leela put the forks in the dishwasher and got out the stuff for baking gingersnaps, while Jay helped Dad to a chair in the living room and talked to him, telling him stuff about the Layton Mansion, about an exotic animal—a liger—he'd treated during his clinicals, about a horse he'd ridden in a race once. Dad didn't respond verbally, of course. However, when Leela peeked in, she saw a light dancing in Dad's blue eyes. They were a lot brighter than usual.

Jay had reignited a long-dim spark.

Jay. Jay Wilson.

But he was leaving Massey Falls at the first possible moment. A tiny knife twisted in her heart.

Dad got settled in front of the TV for his favorite police mystery show, and Jay came into the kitchen, where Leela had stuff all set.

"Ready to make cookies?" She tossed Jay an apron and steeled her gut. "I have a confession to make."

She had to tell him about promising the Layton Mansion this afternoon.

"A confession?" Jay's eyebrow shot upward as he finished tying his apron strings. His shoulders looked so broad by contrast beneath the red fabric. "Is this like truth or dare? 'Cause I'm game. Truth."

She lost her nerve. "These are the only good cookies I can make." She was a rotten, terrible, deceitful chicken!

"You told me that before, but I must say, I don't believe you."

"You should." She listed her failures on her fingers. "First there were the english lemon tea cakes, and then the danish wedding cookies, and then the norwegian *krumkaker*, and then the chinese fortune cookies. Disasters, every one of them."

"Maybe you should have stayed in America. Gingersnaps are American."

But she was still ranting, fueled by her shame at not telling him the real confession on her conscience. "With all the flour I dumped in the trash, I could be sanctioned by the U.N. for waste of finite resources that could have been used to feed a starving nation."

"Please. It's probably just your recipes. Were they smudged? Did you misread them?"

Come to think of it, most of the failed attempts *had* involved smudges. "The results were too consistently bad to blame the recipes themselves. It has to be operator error. Thus, we're sticking with gingersnaps."

"Fine by me." Jay pulled some glasses from his pocket and put them on. "Where do we start?"

Four cups of flour, two cups of sugar, a bottle of molasses, *so* much butter, and an array of spices and leavening agents later, a mixing bowl of dark batter beckoned on the counter.

"Truth or dare again." Leela wiped her hands on a towel. "Are you ready?"

"Always." Jay leaned against the counter. "Okay, truth."

"Do you eat the raw cookie dough, or not?"

"Why do I feel like this is a make-or-break moment?" He looked good without glasses, but even better with them. Brilliant, scholarly, in charge.

Speaking of *charge*, one was surging through Leela right now at the sight of him. "I'm not saying it's make-or-break. Not necessarily."

"Let's do it this way, then." Jay opened the silverware drawer and pulled out a spoon. He dipped it into the batter bowl, pulling out a small mound of dough, his eye sparking. "I'll hold it right … here." He held it out, but not too far.

"Okay." What was he trying to prove with this—this holding the spoon like it was a baited hook, but looking past it like he was ready to devour her instead of the dough?

Leela had to bite her lower lip to keep her chemistry in check. She inched toward him as he pulled the spoon closer to himself. "It's a moving target, and …?"

"Mutual truth or dare here." Jay took Leela's hand, tugging her toward him. The spoon he held out to the side, halfway between their faces. "If in truth I'm a raw cookie dough eater, I'll dare go for it. If you are, you will."

She stood practically toe to toe with him. Jay suspended the spoon between their mouths. His mouth inched toward the spoon, but she hung back, watching, their eyes flicking between each other's gazes and the spoon. Tension spooled in her.

He made another move. "If you want some, maybe you should beat me to it. If I'm a raw dough eater, I'll take it all, you know."

"That is so not happening," she whispered, and in a flash she went for the spoon.

Jay went for it at the same time. Their lips met on the spoon, which only blocked their way for a split second. The second his lower lip brushed hers, their shoulders touched. She felt his body loosen, and he dropped the spoon. It clattered on the tile.

Leela hardly heard it. Ginger and spice and sugar mingled in her senses. His mouth was a satin ribbon tied on the gift of his kiss. He cupped her chin and brushed a thumb across her cheek, while she dissolved in crystallized tingles of longing.

His kiss swept her from the warm kitchen to the North Pole, with a full view of Santa's workshop, where all the good surprises were being fashioned for future happiness. Jay Wilson's kiss comprised her entire wish list, as he let it linger, tease, and dominate her every sense.

"Wow," she said coming up for breath. "You really know how to eat cookie dough."

"It's because you really know how to make cookie dough I can't resist." He wore a glazed expression and spoke in a low, husky voice.

"Is that so?" Her own voice had gone smoky.

Jay proved it a few more times over the next minutes, with kiss after spicy-sweet kiss, her back against the kitchen counter and her soul hovering somewhere between the clouds that hung low and threat'ning and the new fallen snow.

"Truth?" Jay pressed a kiss to each of her eyelids. He must still be playing that truth or dare game from earlier. "I've been wanting to do that for a long, long time."

"A long time? But we just met."

"Seems like ages."

Yeah, it did feel that way. "Truth?" she asked. "When we first talked, I felt like I'd always known you."

"Maybe our moms' wish had something to do with that." He trailed a little line of kisses along her jaw line. "Yeah, I know it's impossible. But stranger things have happened."

"Does this mean you'll take me to the Holiday Ball?"

"If you'll kiss me like this when the clock strikes midnight."

"Guaranteed."

"I like our system of guarantees." He placed another kiss on her lips that caused Leela to spin through dress after dress in her closet. The green velvet gown whispered, *Jay will like this.*

Speaking of midnight, the clock in the living room struck a late hour. Any later, and Leela's judgment would get impaired, especially if she was operating under the influence of Jay's intoxicating kiss.

"If I'm going to get up early and help you in the attic, we'd better say good night."

"You'll come again tomorrow, then? Your family's good will hasn't run out yet?"

"And the next day, and the next. If you want me, that is," Leela said.

"Oh, I want you." Jay's eyes were half-closed. "I mean, to help me with the attic project."

Right. She knew what he meant because the blood in her veins raced in the same direction as his.

"But what about the cookie dough?" he asked. "We haven't baked it yet. We could put some in the oven, think of something to do while we wait for them to bake. Something productive." He had a kiss-glint in his eye.

"Tempting as that is, I'd better put it in the freezer for now. Then I can bake it fresh on the morning of the bake sale." She still hadn't told him the truth about the Cookie House. She had to, or he was going to see his address on the fliers all over town.

Tomorrow. She'd tell him tomorrow. "I'll see you at the crack of dawn."

Chapter 14

Jay

The next morning dawned much colder than those of his previous days in Massey Falls. And Jay was standing out in it, just to cool his irritation caused by this phone call.

"Yeah, you do always call early, Rance. But it's okay. I'm up." Jay paced back and forth on the porch of the Layton Mansion to keep warm while he waited for Leela to appear. He'd fallen asleep last night with the memory of her in his arms, and he'd awakened cold to the reality that she didn't await him at close proximity.

How could he have fallen so far so fast for this girl?

Because she fills my lonely spaces.

And because she was beautiful, kind, and the first person he'd ever told about his mom's life.

Leela Miller could be the girl he'd been looking for. It was far, far too soon to know this—but it was like as a kid, when he'd known he was going to be a vet after the first time seeing a colt born during a difficult delivery. Both mare and colt nearly died, but the doctor had saved them with his quick thinking.

In one short blast of experience, all other possible professions had fallen away from Jay's possibility list.

One short blast of experience with Leela, and any other woman he'd ever known wafted away like so much mist.

And so he knew. He did. *Truth.* Admitting it was like taking a dare.

His breath steamed here on the porch. "I am glad to hear you have other offers for the practice. No, I'm not going to have the money any sooner than I said." Why were Foster & Cody pressuring him so much? What was the rush?

"Yes, I appreciate that you're holding the spot for me." Naturally, they had to, as it was in their signed contract for the option. "I have to go." Leela's car had pulled up to the curb. "No, I'm not trying to delay. Your clients are trying to accelerate the process. That is a totally different thing." His teeth had turned to chalk, and the sun wasn't even up yet. "Yes, I know the price. I'll have it by the third Tuesday. I promise."

Promise! How had he dared promise? No actual offer for sale had come in. He hadn't even put the house on the market officially—because he wasn't even done with the attic yet. Burt's ethereal cash offer people might just be hype, for all Jay knew.

"Hey, there." Leela carried two cups on a tray and what looked like a gift bag. Hearing her voice, Jay's irritation at Rance the broker drained away. "I hope you like cinnamon rolls."

"Did you bake them?"

"Heck, no! These are from the coffee shop. They go well with hot cocoa. You skipped breakfast, I'll bet."

"You'd win that bet. Come on inside." A gust of air from the opening door hit the fireplace, and it crackled. Lit only by the orange glow of the blaze, the room was dim, warm, and inviting.

"You lit a fire again." She rushed toward the hearth and turned to face him, her eyes bright as ever. "This room was made for firelight."

Yeah, well, she'd been the one who lit a fire.

"I thought it needed some seating." He gestured for her to join him on a loveseat. "I found it in the shed out back and dragged it in." The firewood pile was stacked against the shed, and he'd peered in the window and seen the couch. "Just in case you want to warm yourself before we start upstairs."

Or in case she wanted to cozy up beside him a while until the attic warmed up.

"This was in the shed?" Leela handed him the tray and sack while she slipped out of her coat. She was wearing one of those curve-highlighting sweaters again. He had to clench his teeth to keep his jaw from hanging slack.

"The shed? Yeah, there seems to be a lot of stuff out there."

"Do we have to clear that out as well? Or did your Uncle Jingo only care about the attic?"

"Thankfully, the attic was his sole stipulation."

Here she sat by him, filling up all his senses with her cinnamon and chocolate—and her touch. Oh, the suppleness of her body beside his. He could get very used to it.

"It's just like I dreamed as a girl." Reflected firelight danced across her skin. She nestled under his arm and they sipped their cocoa. Her stockinged feet rested on top of his. Everything was warm. "Big tree over there, fire over here, a piano, a big dog curled up on the rug in front of the grate. And the kids all sliding down the banister."

He could see it. He didn't even have to close his eyes. The vision of it unfolded in vivid detail: kids laughing and bickering about whose turn it was, badly played carols on the piano, the smell of the pine from the tree.

"You imagined all of that as a girl?"

"Girls have good imaginations."

Or maybe girls had the gift of prophecy. Like both their moms had attempted in that compact they'd written.

If I decided differently. If instead I stayed ...

No. Nope. He was selling the Layton Mansion. He was getting his job. He'd planned his work, and now he was working his plan.

For heaven's sake, he'd just made a verbal promise to deliver the asking price to Foster & Cody not fifteen minutes ago.

Even if it meant he wasn't going to see his children sliding down that newly sanded, stained, and varnished banister. Or if it meant he wasn't going to let a dog curl up on the rug beside the flame or listen to carols and laughter alongside a gorgeous girl with a heart of gold. He was committed. He would sell this place and use the money to buy a partnership in Precious Companion.

Leela rested her head against his chest.

Precious Companion. It didn't sound nearly as precious in that moment.

***

Halfway through their day in the attic, Leela's phone started blowing up with texts.

Jay set down his box of tarnished silver candlesticks. "What's going on? Is your dad okay?" He shouldn't be keeping her here day after day. It was utterly selfish, and he knew it. But he wanted her, and she'd reassured him that Mr. Miller was being well cared for by yet another cousin. Christmastime service, willingly given, she'd said. "Do you need to go? I can come with you to check on him."

Leela put her phone back in her pocket. "Oh, no. Yeah. He's fine. I just have a ton of cousins in general. There's always some kind of group text attacking all our phones." She dusted off a top of a box. "Hey, actually"—she held out her screen to him—"check this out. It's right within your area of expertise. They're from Pippa, mostly. She's the one who married Dr. Harrison's son."

The phone screen told a veterinarian's worst nightmare: a horse with broken leg.

New texts popped in from Leela's cousin Pippa.

And now, Chub says his dad isn't sure Rose Red is going to make it.

Rose Red! "The prize-winning thoroughbred?" he asked, and Leela nodded gravely.

It's too much pressure for Chub's dad. He's telling Bing Whitmore to take Rose Red to Reedsville, but with the snow, it's a basically guaranteed loss. Bing lost Snow White last summer. If he loses Rose

Red, I don't know what will happen to the stables.

"What do you think, Jay? Is there any chance?"

"I haven't seen the injury, obviously, but the demands on a performance horse make fractures really common. I doubt the horse's career can be saved." Jay had to tell the truth. "Its life may even be in question. A lot of owners would put it down."

"Its life!" Leela took the phone back. "I didn't realize its life was on the line!" The way her whole body tensed, Jay knew this horse she'd never even seen in person suddenly mattered very much to her.

"If you like, I can go over there. Offer to help."

"Would you? Oh, Jay! Please?"

"Um …" It wasn't any of his business, but how could he deny her anything when she looked at him with those blue eyes brimming? "Can you check with your cousin to find out if my offer would be welcome?"

***

"It's a compound break." In the chilly air of Whitmore Thoroughbred's stables, Dr. Harrison pointed to the obvious break on Rose Red's leg for Jay to examine. Yeah, severe and complex. "It's such a shame."

The air in the stables smelled like straw, feed, and leather—nature's most perfect blend of scents. Jay inhaled deeply, not even minding the added horse manure mixed in, to clear his mind to think. Crazy as it might sound to anyone else, the smells around animals were half the reason he'd wanted to become a vet.

However, a situation like this was half the reason he'd dreaded becoming one. No one wanted to lose a beloved animal. Especially not one worth an enormous investment.

"So, there's nothing you can do?" Bing Whitmore put his head in his hands. The guy was a lot younger than Jay had anticipated. In Jay's experience, thoroughbred owners were usually middle-aged guys who drove Jaguars and drank wines of good vintage. This guy was no older than Jay—and he looked as broken about the possible loss of this horse as Rose Red's broken leg. "Nothing at all?"

85

Dr. Harrison shook his head. "You were wise not to let her walk on it, but it might not be enough precaution. I can splint with boards and PVC pipe, but if she walks again, she'll put too much weight on it. She'd have to more or less be in traction until it heals. That's no good for her."

Jay was nothing but an interloper here, at Leela's request. He shouldn't speak up. But then Leela pulled on his coat sleeve. "Please, Jay? Can't you help Bing? Isn't there some way to save Rose Red?"

"There could be a way," he whispered. But how could he make a suggestion and not sound like some young upstart meddler? Dr. Harrison knew his business. Jay shouldn't butt in. "It's a long shot."

"Then tell Dr. Harrison. Tell Bing Whitmore." Leela's voice pitched upward. "A life is at stake here."

Jay cleared his throat. "While I was in vet school, I was given a chance to assist in a surgery where a horse had a break similar to this."

"You were?" Bing lifted his head from his hands. "Dr. Harrison—who is this guy?"

"Just met him. New veterinary graduate. He's got roots here, but he's taking a job over in Reedsville. Small animal."

"Oh. Small animal." Bing visibly deflated. "I guess equine surgery isn't your wheelhouse." He collapsed against the rails of the stall again.

"I have experience in both. It's limited, mind you." Extremely. Which about killed him right now. "But the vet I assisted used metal screws inserted both above and below a similar fracture to Rose Red's in order to save the horse's leg."

And life, he could have added.

Leela let out a soft cry, which she muffled by shoving her hand across her mouth.

"I don't have a full surgical setup, I'm afraid." Dr. Harrison shook his head. "Anesthesia, some, and a basic kit, but that's it."

"This veterinary surgeon performed the operation in the field, actually." Yeah, it sounded insane. Jay had thought so at the time, too. Complex surgeries should be done in sterile environments with controlled, well, everything. "The pins had to be extremely strong to hold the horse's weight, and that required drilling."

"Drilling!" Leela gasped. "With a drill?"

"I have a drill in the shop." Bing's voice was a thread. This mattered to him, and it was starting to matter more and more to Jay.

The shop drill would do in a pinch. As would the supply of anesthetics Dr. Harrison had in his kit.

"But how were the results?" Bing asked.

"The horse wasn't perfect, but it lived."

"It was lame." Dr. Harrison didn't sound convinced. He turned to Bing. "A lame horse …"

"Is a live horse," Bing said firmly and stepped toward Jay. "Could you repeat the surgery? Is it possible?"

"I was only assisting. And you must realize that even if the surgery is effective, bone density will be lost, and the leg will be prone to re-fracture."

Bing pressed his hands together, and then he ran his fingers through his hair. "Here's how I see it. You don't try, and we have to put Rose Red down. You do try, and we might save her. If there's even a small chance of that, it's not even a discussion."

Jay turned to Dr. Harrison, not sure whether to ask permission or to override the older man's authority here. But Dr. Harrison's white swirl of hair bobbed a go-ahead.

"You can use my surgical tools from the truck. Let's get started right away."

Chapter 15

Leela

Another cold, dust-filled day passed in the attic with Jay, now known to her and the Whitmores as the savior of a famous horse's life. Jay had done it. With Dr. Harrison's help, of course—lots of it. Bing Whitmore had performed a nurse's duties of handing the surgeons items while Leela had prayed.

In the end, Rose Red's leg was set, and she might make it. If she didn't, at least they'd given everything they could in the moment.

When the last stitch was tied, Bing had hugged Jay. *Thanks, brother. We love this horse.*

Jay had taken Leela home. She'd kissed her hero tenderly, just like he'd treated Rose Red in her time of pain.

Tenderly.

And now, here they were in the attic again, another day turned to nighttime.

Today, Leela was practically hoarse from laughing and talking so much. They'd even done a karaoke sing-off of their favorite Christmas carols for half the afternoon. Holy wassails, Batman! That guy knew a never-ending list of carols. She'd run out of songs long before Jay had.

"I've got dinner cooking in the crock pot at my house, if you're interested," she said as they descended the stairs together. "I don't want to monopolize your time, though."

"But I *want* you to monopolize my time." On the landing of the second floor, he took her in his arms. She got so dizzy from this kiss, she wasn't sure if they were falling down the stairs or floating up to the ceiling. He unhinged her more with every show of affection.

Which were getting more and more frequent. And the work in the attic getting less and less efficient as a result.

Nothing had gone too far, but she would definitely need to fix her ponytail before she set foot outside the Layton Mansion into full view of Society Row.

"The thing I'm worried about is monopolizing *your* time. How are you going to finish planning your fundraiser?"

Oh, that. She really should be organizing what was left of her responsibilities. Una Mae would expect another report tomorrow, and she'd contacted Leela with a new demand: decorations for the Holiday Ball. *They're at the same venue. No sense decorating twice.*

So far, Jay must not have seen or heard the advertising. He hadn't said anything. But Leela had seen it—all over town. There was even a banner draped between street lights on Main Street.

This was getting critical. "I need to tell you something about the Cookie House."

"That it's the same day as the Holiday Ball? I need to know the color of your dress, for sure. Is there some kind of matching wardrobe expectation for dates?"

There was. "I'm probably going to be in dark green velvet."

He ran his hand over her waist to her hip. "That will be very, very nice." He leaned in and kissed her, and she lost her nerve again for now. "What do you have left to prepare?"

"Decorations."

"For the cookie fundraiser or the ball?"

"Both." The weight of it pressed down like a vise. She hadn't even *begun* to amass the piles and piles of decorations she'd need to make this event happen. All she had found were some sad, ratty garlands in a box of Mom's stuff.

Instead, she'd been idling away her time in an attic and making nightly batches of cookie dough to share off spoons with Jay Wilson, raw-cookie-dough-eater extraordinaire.

"What can I do to help you with the project?"

What man ever asked that? Now was the perfect time to tell him about the location being, well, his house. "Unless you know where to get a thousand piles of vintage Christmas decorations, probably nothing."

If she told him that the event had been announced, he might react badly. He might not trust her—even though she didn't deserve his trust at this point.

She kicked the conversation down the road, like the yellow-bellied coward she was.

"What do they usually use? Can't you use those?"

"In the past it's been Una Mae Coldicott's décor. The Coldicotts have an extravaganza of Rudolph the Red-Nosed Reindeer-themed decorations. It's like being in the TV special when you walk into wherever the Cookie House is being held."

"Is everyone required to pretend they're doing stop-motion animation as they go through?" He mimed the stilted, robotic movements as he came in for another kiss.

Leela laughed through the mash of his lips on hers. "She's holding them hostage this year. No Rudolph."

"What's her problem with you, anyway?"

Should she tell him this gem from her life? "It's because I won't date her lecherous son Felix."

"Felix? Coldicott? Big guy, small round glasses, slicked-back oily hair? Looks like that Ricky guy from the eighties movie with John Cusack?" That was the one. "I met him at the barber shop last month. Seems like he borders on feral, if his conversation that day was any indicator."

"Precisely. And Una Mae's holding the use of her house and Rudolph and the sleigh and the whole island of misfit toys hostage until

I agree to go with Felix to the Holiday Ball."

Uh-oh. The whole truth had nearly come out. Well, three-fourths had.

Jay brushed some hair from Leela's face. "Could you just tell everyone you have a boyfriend? It's usually an iron-clad excuse."

"Felix Coldicott is not my boyfriend."

Now Jay laughed. "I meant *me.*"

"Oh."

"That's all you've got to say? Is *oh?*"

"No, I have this to say." Leela should have said, *I told them I was having the Cookie House here.* Instead she kissed him and said, "I'd love to tell everyone you're my boyfriend."

Chapter 16

Jay

A full week into their attic project, and the halfway mark still looked like it was a stone's throw away. *Speaking of throw away...* Jay was ready to chuck every single box of Uncle Jingo's collection again to get things moving on his life and toward his goals.

But maybe not the goals he'd been thinking of for the past several months.

If it hadn't provided the perfect excuse for taking every second of Leela Miller's days, he would have burned all of it, Uncle Jingo's contingencies be blazed.

Then, when he'd made his first doctor's fee for operating on a rich person's Persian cat's failing liver, it would all be worth it.

Cat livers.

Cat livers were his future. Unless …

Performing that horse surgery was amazing. It might not hurt to have a backup plan if Foster and Cody didn't work out. Even if it the backup too was pie-in-the-sky dreaming.

"I'm going downstairs to make a quick phone call." Jay abandoned Leela in the attic and dialed Mr. Overson—Dr. Harrison's business manager—who had been frustratingly elusive. A voice came through on the other side, and Jay sped down the stairs to the first floor to start the conversation.

"Mr. Overson?"

"I don't recognize this number. Who's calling?"

Jay introduced himself.

"Oh, yes. Dr. Wilson. I heard about you. Horse surgeon. Innovator. Well, I was out on the ranch until yesterday, incommunicado, so I didn't get back to you. But yes, Dr. Harrison is interested in looking toward retirement. At that time he would plan to sell his practice, naturally. Are you interested?"

That depended. "Can you give me a ballpark on the purchase price?"

Overson named an exorbitant sum. Jay tried to keep his choke inaudible. It was multiple times the value of the Layton House. Much more than the partnership buy-in at Precious Companion.

"Dr. Wilson? Are you still there?"

"Uh, yeah." But he was stunned into silence.

"It's a valuable practice, worth every cent. And a great life, especially if you want to set up shop in a town like Massey Falls."

"Thank you for your information."

"Thanks for the interest."

Vague, lookie-loo interest was the only thing Jay could give at that price. They hung up.

Jay plodded back up the stairs to where Leela was still at work—getting ready to sell the house right out from under her event.

With all the kissing distractions of late, Jay still hadn't discussed with Burt a contingency clause for whomever might buy it. He should do that right now. He fired off a text. *Burt, can we talk about building in a contingency clause to the sale so that the Cookie House can happen here at the mansion?*

Nothing came back immediately. Jay looked around, less enthusiastic to complete the task. Had they even touched the stacks? There looked to be twice as many as when they started.

"What number are we on?" Leela held the sharpie marker perched above their just-completed box. "Two eighty-three?"

"Three eighty-four."

"Is it that many already?"

"Already? Seems like a thousand at this point. And we haven't found much of value. Unless you count a few decorative items that could be worth something if I bother to get them appraised instead of hauling them to the thrift store."

"You've shown the partially complete inventory list to the lawyer to send to your relatives? Do any of them want anything?"

"Nobody's responded to anything on any list." Not even Mom. In fact, she wouldn't even look at the list when he sent her a photo of it. *Not my circus, not my monkeys,* she'd said.

Circus was pretty accurate. This mess could have been created by hyperactive monkeys let out of their cages.

Leela's brightness hadn't dimmed, though, despite Jay's trip into the dumps.

"At least get that egg-shaped thing and the little stand appraised. It looks valuable. I think I remember my mom showing me a photo of something like it in a magazine once. The filigree on it might at least be real gold."

Appraisals. Filigree. Hundreds more boxes to go. Nobody wanted any of this stuff. Not even Jay.

Plus, he was never going to make his deadline.

"Why do you want in to the Ladies' Auxiliary so much?"

"My mom was in it." Leela stiffened. "And because they do a lot of good work."

"There are lots of ways to do good work."

"Not in this town. There's only the Ladies' Auxiliary."

Jay doubted that. "Not *only* the Ladies' Auxiliary, surely."

"If you want to do the most—like helping every citizen from the infants to the elderly—you go with established channels. In Massey Falls, the Ladies' Auxiliary is *the* established channel. They're rife with potential, like a sleeping giant, ready to dig in and perform any great good. I hope they let me in."

What kind of idiots wouldn't let Leela Miller into their club? "Why shouldn't everyone be allowed to join, if it's truly a service organization?"

"It's the way things are done. Which is why I volunteered to chair their biggest fundraiser of the year. I wanted to prove I've got potential."

Right. Right. "You're keeping your mom's legacy alive."

"Yeah. I hope so." She clouded for a second, but then composed herself. "Look, I know I've said this too many times before, but the Layton Mansion really is key, not just to the event but to my getting into the organization. Everyone wants to see inside it, since it's been shut up so long."

Maybe he should just let her use the mansion, whether or not the attic was finished. She needed it. "Leela, I—"

"So I did something terrible, Jay."

"You did?"

She worried her lower lip between her teeth. "I told the Ladies' Auxiliary I was in negotiations to use the Layton Mansion."

"You did?" What was so wrong with that? "That's true enough."

"I also ..." She looked at the ceiling, and then she met his eyes. "I told them you said yes."

"Oh."

"At which point, they printed fliers. They bought ads for the radio. They announced it on social media as the venue for both the Cookie House and the Holiday Ball. It's the only place in the whole town that could host both."

"They ... announced it?" Jay's voice cracked. This turn of events could potentially sink a sale, especially if it was widely known, which—apparently it was. "Do you have any backup venues?"

She shook her head, fear in her eyes. "I had to, Jay. I—I'm sorry." Her chin quivered and her eyes got glassy. "For advertising. It's coming up so soon. The third Tuesday in December looms only days away now."

As if Jay didn't know that fact. "We're not done with the attic."

"It seemed so close. You did say we had a deal if …"

Yeah, he had said there was a deal. She was right. And she'd spent every single day helping him prepare the attic for the house to sell. What kind of a jerk would it make him if he said no now? He exhaled, stirring dust up into the air in a swirl.

The two big events that were hitting that fated day sparked with friction of flint and steel, threatening to burn each other down.

And there was a bigger problem with saying yes to Leela: with no response yet from Burt, he hadn't put in place any contingency for delay if a buyer came forward.

The tension had been eating him alive, but he had managed until now to push the actual discussion into the future. Without completing the attic, the point had been moot. But now, time was crushing them both. Unless he sold, he could lose his shot at the Reedsville clinic. Clearly, he could never afford to buy Dr. Harrison's practice. But if he sold, he'd pull the rug out from under Leela.

She looked so forlorn, and he was no monster. Yeah, she should have told him sooner, but the damage was done. He could either flip out or roll with the situation.

"It's going to be okay." He rested a hand on her shoulder. "I think."

"Are you sure, Jay? I feel horrible. I'm so sorry. I knew we had a deal and that I hadn't helped you finish. I don't blame you if you're upset."

Was he upset? Yeah, but not exactly about what Leela had done. More about what all the separate waves combining into one giant rogue wave were doing to his life.

"You're quiet. I get it. I can go. We can cancel it or book the library's conference room. It won't be nearly as cool, but I'll fix it. I'm so sorry."

"Leela," he said. She was melting before his eyes. Jay took her in his arms. "It's probably going to be fine."

After all, the attic wasn't done, per Uncle Jingo's stipulation, nor was there a buyer on the hook. It would probably be fine.

A loud knocking sounded downstairs. "Yo! Jay? I saw your car on the street. You in here?" The voice, though muffled, was intelligible. Burt Basingstoke.

"Is that Emily's dad?" Leela asked, looking up from a particularly cobweb-infested box. A patch of dust rested on her cheek. Jay wiped it off with his thumb.

"I think so. I'll go down."

"I'll come, too. He's my cousin-in-law, after all."

"You don't have to." Jay still hadn't told her about that possible cash buyer or the lack of a built-in contingency for taking possession of the house.

Burt's bombastic voice thundered from the bottom of the attic stairs. "Jay, my boy! Come on down here. Excellent news! I have a buyer for you. Cash. They're here now, ready as rain in a heavy thundercloud."

Chapter 17

Jay

"R eady?" What did Burt mean, ready? "We're not done with the attic."

Jay and Leela descended the stairs and met Burt in the kitchen. It was colder down here.

"Oh, hey there, Leela. Didn't expect to run into you here. Of course, it makes sense now, what Emily said when she told me you were falling crazy-dog in love with someone. Might as well be with the heir of all this property. This smarty-pants young man is going to be rich, rich, rich in a few minutes, and he won't even have to bear the burden of this old place, come nightfall."

In love! Jay shot a glance at Leela's reddening face. She pressed a hand to her cheek for a second and bit her lower lip before turning to her cousin's husband with a retort.

"What are you talking about, Burt?" Leela asked. "Jay's not selling yet."

"Yeah," Jay said scuffing his toe across the wood floor. "Turns out the Layton Mansion is going to be this year's Cookie House, and also host the Holiday Ball."

"Yeah, on Tuesday, a week from today," Leela said.

"Not if Jay is as smart as I think he is." Burt winked at Leela. She recoiled and then looked at Jay, her eyes shouting questions at him.

I could have so easily prevented this situation.

"Did you get my message?" Jay stepped toward Burt, with Leela behind him, as if Jay could shield her from all this destruction. "About adding a stipulation allowing the Ladies' Auxiliary to use the house?"

It was as if Burt hadn't heard. "The buyers are outside and will be coming in any second. They're chomping at the bit!" Burt grinned, showing too many of his back teeth.

"Burt, there are some complications."

Snowplowing on, Burt said, "Speaking of Ladies' Auxiliary—by wild coincidence, the buyers just happen to be the Coldicott family. Una Mae is one of your Ladies' Auxiliary cohorts, isn't she, Leela?"

Leela gave a sharp intake of breath and grabbed Jay's elbow.

Everyone was talking at once.

"Jay, she's—"

"Burt, there's something you need to—"

"I hear Mrs. Coldicott is the Ladies' Auxiliary's grand poobah, or whatever they call women. Poobette?" Burt let out a guffaw.

"At least the first syllable of that nickname applies," Leela muttered.

"Please. Burt. Did you let the buyers know about the third Tuesday stipulation?" Jay had to get a word in. "I texted you requesting we write in a delay contingency for the Cookie House."

"Of course they'll be amenable. She's in the Ladies' Auxiliary!"

Leela and Jay exchanged glances. Jay stepped toward Burt again. "You've got it in writing, then?"

"Not yet. Nothing's in writing yet. Nothing's signed. But I have no doubts. None at all. She came, cash in hand." His eyes flashed dollar signs.

Leela let out a little cry of despair.

"She's anxious to get the deal done. Buying it for the son."

Ew. Feral Felix would have *his* children sliding down the banister Jay had restored?

Burt lowered his voice. "I'm guessing it's so he'll move out of their basement after all this time." He curled his fingers and blew on his nails, then he rubbed them on his collar as if he'd won the Masters' Tournament. "When I told them about all the remodeling work you'd done and that you were clearing out that attic, you should've seen the way old Mrs. Coldicott lit up. Like the Christmas tree ceremony on town square. Shazowie! It was like a race to the family treasure chest of gold buried in the back yard. They couldn't hurry down here fast enough."

"Speaking of the attic." Jay had to put the brakes on this until the Cookie House delay was in writing. Leela was shaking beside him. "But what about the clean-out stipulation in the will? It has to be completed, right? Legally?"

Some of Burt's hot air deflated. "That'll have to be gotten around, of course." He puffed back up again, salesman-grinning. "But I'm sure we can figure things out with the contract. They seem *very* anxious to buy. I mentioned the attic wasn't done, and they say they don't care. In fact, they even offered to finish the inventory job themselves if you want."

Well, Jay didn't want to inventory another box of junk for as long as he lived, but it didn't seem right to give family items to strangers all of a sudden. What if there were another diary up there? Or more of Mom's past? Maybe Uncle Jingo's stipulation had been wise after all.

Besides, this wasn't going to work anyway. There was no clear view through the legal haze. Or the Cookie House haze. He turned to ask Leela what she thought, but all that remained of her was a click of the door to the attic, and the hollow tread of footsteps across its wood floors above.

Chapter 18

Leela

Ooh, that Una Mae! And her good-for-nothing son Felix! How could they swoop in like that and buy the house right out from under the Cookie House event? No way would they allow it to be used if they owned it. Make that no way would they allow Leela to succeed.

What was all the point of this vindictive behavior? Leela had never once done anything to encourage Felix, make him think she was interested. Sure, she'd always been cordial when Una Mae brought him to events, but she'd never flirted. Heavens, no. They couldn't have any complaints on those grounds.

Besides, what they were doing now amounted to persecution!

Leela scraped her fingernails across the plaster of the attic's wall.

Those anti-cookie control freaks! Whatever made Una Mae tick? And why had she chosen Leela as her Christmas terrorism project this year?

The upshot was this: Cookie House at Layton Mansion was doomed. As was Leela's shot at being Mom's heir in the community service world. That dream dried up and shattered, like last month's leaf crunched underfoot on a busy sidewalk.

And what about Burt for being so obtuse? How could he declare right in front of Jay that Leela was in love? Didn't he know anything about a tender plant and not to shine too much sun on it or it might burn up?

The dingbat. Obtuse happily married person who'd forgotten how fragile a work it was to foster a new relationship.

Now Jay would be all awkward around her. She'd seen the look on his face during Burt's big announcement of Leela's love. He'd looked more stunned than pleased.

Scattered contents of boxes and futility and broken hope spilled everywhere around her.

The whole world was pretty much chucking her over. From Blaine, to losing Mom, to watching the one guy she'd ever really connected with more or less sell her out.

Why, Universe? Why let her come *this* close to having something like keeping the Cookie House alive in Mom's honor—and then swat it away? Why let her start to think she had a boyfriend, only to send him off to the one city she refused to live in ever again? Not that she could leave Massey Falls even if she wanted to, considering her family responsibilities.

Jay would be out of here before the ink dried on the contract.

Jay Wilson was leaving.

Just like everyone else.

Hot tears streamed down her cheeks, scorching trails through the dust on her skin.

When he left, it was over for her and Jay. Leela wasn't naïve. Long distance relationships struggled for oxygen. No way could she move to Reedsville, not with Dad's state. He needed to be in a familiar place. And Jay couldn't commute two hours each way every day. Not if he wanted to fully invest in his career. Nor if he wanted to fully invest in a relationship.

Leela wouldn't ask him to give up what he'd worked and borrowed and studied for his whole life.

Frustration sent her toward another box. She tipped it to see inside. *Fragile* was written on the side of the box in a spidery hand. *Plink-*

plink. She lifted it carefully from the top of the stack, and moved it under the light bulb.

Inside lay wads of tissue paper, but … plinking? Leela carefully unwrapped one wad.

Good honk! What was this? A frosted glass ball of the most delicate structure rested in her hand. Gold glass, yes, but silver glitter ran in ridges from pole to pole.

A paper was tucked up against the side of the box. Leela set down the gem and picked up the folded sheet.

My great-grandmother's Christmas tree never lacked for beauty. These are a sample of her best items, which she purchased during a trip to London in the late 1880s. All the other decorating for her home here in Massey Falls is tucked away in the loft of the shed out back.

My regret is never using them to restore Layton Mansion to its Christmas glory. And now I'm too feeble to do so. –Hildy Layton Charles

Leela had no idea who Hildy Layton Charles was, but the contents of this box hinted at a treasure trove of Victorian Christmas decorations not in this attic but in the loft of the shed.

If only the Cookie House were still being held here in the Layton Mansion, it wouldn't even need any of stingy Una Mae's Rudolph decorations. In fact, everything Leela needed might all be sourced right here—authentic and beautiful and cherished.

If only I could have used them, I would have been fulfilling a wish for Hildy Layton Charles. A woman Leela had never met, but whom she could still serve and honor. If the Cookie House plan weren't defunct.

How perfectly sad the timing!

Because Jay was busy selling this gorgeous house and everything in it to stingy Una Mae and the King of the Island of Misfit Toys.

What vendetta was she pursuing? It couldn't all be tied to Leela's rejection of Felix. No, this revenge mentality had to stem from deeper roots. *Did it stretch back to Mom?* No, not a chance. Mom had been an angel to everyone. Of course, devils hated angels …

Somehow Leela had to get to the bottom of it.

And the Cookie House was still going to happen this year.

A strength coiled up from the bottom of Leela's toes and rose through her legs, torso, and neck. She stood tall, her spine straight, and her fists clenching and unclenching as she descended the stairs.

Whatever was with Una Mae and her vendetta, it ended now.

Chapter 19

Jay

A stack of hundred-dollar bills gleamed at Jay from the granite countertop. A breeze from the ceiling fan fluttered the edges of the top two notes, begging him, *Take me. I'm yours.*

"As soon as Burt here irons out the contractual wrinkle about the attic clean-out, all this money is yours, and the sooner the better." Mrs. Coldicott lived up to the first syllable in her last name. Brrr. The son sniveled beside her.

Finally, Jay got it about Leela's word *icky*. This Felix dude embodied it. Jay kept a safe distance from the aura of pure ickiness rolling off the guy.

Something felt off, definitely. *Why is she so anxious to buy the place?*

Rumblings of understanding sounded in the distance of Jay's gut, but he couldn't decipher them yet.

"You said you wanted to find a buyer as quickly as possible." Burt sounded almost apologetic. "I always try to serve my clients' stated wishes."

But not always their best interests. That was the silent part of Burt's meaning.

Burt left to go type up the sales contract at his office. He'd be back. "Burt—" Jay called. Too late.

"Meeting your stated wishes is our wish as well." Una Mae Coldicott gave a trilling laugh, like a winter bird. The kind with cold blood. "Isn't it *wonderful* that your wish and ours dovetail so nicely? We can finish all the paperwork and record the title transfer today. Before tea time, even!"

What time was tea time? Or did she mean a golf reference? "The golf course is under three feet of snow."

"Yes, the quicker the better." She acted like he hadn't spoken. "You have things to do and veterinary practices to buy, I hear."

Where would she have heard that? Burt, probably. He was one of those loose cannons rolling around the deck of the warship. Of course, that hadn't been all bad. At least he'd made that off-hand mention of what his daughter had leaked about Leela's feelings for Jay.

Leela loves me? Did a teenager's gossip count? Could just be speculation. *If she does, then ...*

"I'm considering buying into a partnership in Reedsville, yes. But I am keeping all my options open." Not very open, considering the price Harrison was asking for the opportunity to stay in Massey Falls and work with him in the large animal practice. But he hadn't totally let the door slam shut. There were business loans, weren't there? He could finance it.

Maybe.

"Oh, but Dr. Wilson." Una Mae's laugh began to grate. A cheese-grater for his soul. "That pronouncement smacks of cold feet. I'd be much more interested in an immediate sale and possession. It's very important to strike while the iron's hot." She opened one eye much wider than the other. It had a sinister quality. "While the cash is still on the table, so to speak."

She lightly touched the pile of hundred-dollar bills.

Felix plucked a hair out of a mole on his chest and put it in his mouth.

Yeah, Leela should not date that guy.

Jay wasn't ready to pick up the money.

Where was Leela? He could text her discretely. He needed her opinion, although he probably could guess it with very little effort. Pulling out his phone, he scrolled to her photo. *The girl with the rose leaves in her hair.* And the heart big enough for everyone. *Does she care whether I stay or go?*

What if Burt's daughter Emily wasn't exaggerating Leela's feelings for him, and Leela had fallen for him enough to admit it? That could change Jay's trajectory.

Where was she?

Una Mae tapped the pile of bills again. "Time is of the essence, Dr. Wilson."

Felix clicked his tongue in rhythm. Tick-tock.

"The will seemed pretty iron-clad about the attic, if I remember right." Jay could delay things, maybe put the negotiations on hold for a few minutes. Not that the Coldicotts seemed amenable to any postponement in the deal. Burt would be back with printed contracts shortly—and no guarantee the Cookie House delay contingency would even be included.

"I thought you were anxious to sell. Basingstoke led me to believe you were a motivated, discrete seller. If you're not, I'm shocked by your misleading statements to the most respected real estate broker in town." Her brow arched. "You're not a liar, are you?"

No, he wasn't a liar. But he did recognize a bad gut feeling when he got one.

"We have to consider the legalities of the contract."

"Those will be gotten around." Mrs. Coldicott decreed this as if she were the law itself. "In a timely fashion."

"Time is another consideration, Mrs. Coldicott. I've been discussing with Mr. Basingstoke the need to write in a contingency for the sale."

"Contingency?" A dragon awoke in her voice. "I'm not interested in contingencies."

"This is a small concession I would have to ask."

"I don't consider the words small and concession to belong in the same sentence."

I'm sure you don't. But he wouldn't leave Leela high and dry. "Whoever purchases the house would need to wait to take possession after next Tuesday. I have promised the Ladies' Auxiliary here in town the use of the Layton Mansion for their annual fundraiser. The Christmas Cookie House? I'm sure you've heard of it."

"There will be no contingencies, Dr. Wilson." Mrs. Coldicott commenced a stare-down with Jay.

Jay refused to blink. "But I've made commitments. Don't you care about the Cookie House fundraiser? It's vital to the community, you know."

Una Mae was not to be diverted from her barreling course. "This morning, Basingstoke described in detail your commitment to the vet clinic in Reedsville. Thinking of your plight, I leapt immediately to your aid, knowing I was one of the few in town who could help you on such short notice. I'm rescuing your plans, Dr. Wilson. You *are* legitimately trying to enter a career path, are you not?"

The stare-down resumed—until Felix's nasally whine interjected.

"I wish old Basingstoke would get a move on," Felix Coldicott grumbled. He had to be forty, but he slouched like a spoiled teenager. "We heard there's a rotten old egg somewhere in that attic. She don't want anyone else cleaning it out but her. And me."

"Shush, Felix." Una Mae turned a sickly sweet smile toward Jay. "Rotten eggs, really! As if a temporary hint of sulfur could change our mind about buying the house."

Something was definitely fishy.

"Felix?" Jay started to ask.

Una Mae cut him off faster than a vet cuts the umbilical cord of a baby calf. "It's just a local legend my son likes to repeat. Lots of legends about the Laytons. Of course, you've heard them all. They even had that one daughter who"—Una Mae lowered her voice—"had Mayor

Allsbury's baby."

Jay bristled. "Mrs. Coldicott, you do not know what you're talking about."

"Oh, please. Everyone knew about Ceri Layton and her affair with Mayor Allsbury. It's not gossip if it's true."

That was just it—the gossip wasn't true. Not for a red-hot second. "That rumor was nothing but a dirty lie created by that lecher to cover up his bad behavior, and I'll bet you and the rest of the town know it— if you'll examine it without giving his word false clout based on his holding elected office."

"He was a respected man."

"Please! When the populace believed him instead of the innocent girl, her life was ruined. There's a reason she never returned to this town, and it's people like you."

And people like Uncle Jingo who'd refused to come to Mom's defense when the rumors spread like a cancer over her life.

Both Leela's mom and mine have suffered cancer. Just in different forms.

"Oh, grow up, Jay Wilson. I know she's your mother, and you *would* think that. Have you ever had your DNA tested? Are you sure you're not Mayor Allsbury's son?"

Jay swallowed hard so as not to let the bile up his throat. "You don't deserve an explanation." Jay had been born three years after Mom left Massey Falls, never to return. "What ever happened to your precious mayor, eh?"

"He was Daddy's friend. And we don't share negative talk about those we're loyal to." Una Mae looked at her fingernails. Clearly, she knew about the harassment charges for which her precious mayor had been convicted. Not that she cared about them. "You should learn about loyalty to the *right* people, Jay Wilson. So should your girlfriend, and her father—not to mention her mother, the interloper."

Una Mae had something against Leela's mom? Layers were peeling back now, but not enough that Jay could decipher the heart of the poisonous fruit.

"What does the Miller family have to do with anything?" Jay wasn't really asking. He was busy digging his fingernails into the palms of his hands so as not to throw a punch.

"If Freesia Youngblood hadn't been so diehard, so mistakenly steadfast"—Una Mae's eyes rolled far enough she could probably see her frontal lobe—"to Ceri Layton when Ceri was obviously in the wrong, I wouldn't be a Coldicott today. *I'd be a Miller.*"

What the—?

"For some unknown reason, Frank Miller found Freesia Youngblood's so-called noble dedication to a fallen woman to be appealing. He married her instead of me, and she ruined him. Forced him into that lowly profession climbing trees, like some primate. Think of it! The practical demigod Frank Miller, confined to his bed! If he'd married me, he would never be in the state he's in now. Widowed, injured, alone."

Holy smokes, there was animosity decades-deep at play here—in a stack of hundred-dollar bills six inches deep, too.

"Frank Miller is not alone. He has a great daughter." And from what Jay could tell, Frank had had a very happy marriage.

"Freesia was wrong for him! She believed your mother's lies and—"

Footfalls sounded on the stairs. A second later, Leela pushed her way through the kitchen door, her eyes ablaze. "Felix Coldicott. You and your mother had better leave. Now."

Chapter 20

Leela

"I don't know what you're talking about, young lady. You're no part of this discussion. It's a property sale, and you're neither owner nor buyer. So you're the one who had better leave." Una Mae rose to her full height, towering over both her son and Leela.

If looks could wound, Leela would be maiming every Coldicott in this room. "Una Mae Coldicott, you know exactly what you are doing, coming in here and buying the Cookie House before the fundraiser can occur here." Leela would pry out of Una Mae the cause of her persecution, or—

"Hey, guys." Burt banged through the front door, his voice entering the kitchen before he did. "Contract complete! Round of applause, please."

"Why, Jay! The contracts are here." Una Mae turned to Jay just as Burt came in through the front door with paperwork in hand. "I assume you're ready to sign." Una Mae grinned like she'd caught all the insects in Massey Falls in her spidery web. "We'll just pretend our little disagreement of a moment ago never happened. I'm willing to forgive it. Felix would like to move in this evening."

Leela's gut tumbled. This evening! But what about the attic

stipulation, and getting the decorations out of the loft of the shed, and all the preparation for the Cookie House?

She shot a desperate glance at Jay. "You're signing?"

One look at his pleading face and Leela melted. Of course Jay was signing the sale contract. His whole future hung in the balance, all his work and dreams. Leela couldn't stand in his way.

"Leela, I need to talk to—"

"You have to sign. Your whole future depends on it."

And in that version of the future, Felix Coldicott would be the sole inhabitant of this enormous house, and no darling child of Leela's would slide down the beautifully polished banister on Christmas morning. Ever.

So this was how dreams died. On the tip of a ballpoint pen.

"That's right," Una Mae simpered, while her face told that inwardly she cackled in triumph. "I never thought I'd be saying this, but Leela Miller is right, Dr. Wilson. You have your future to think about. And so does she. I know Freesia Youngblood's daughter has always dreamed of this house as being her own, and now that Felix will be its owner, it's within her reach. He's already asked her to the Holiday Ball. Do I sense a declaration in the air?"

A declaration! "I didn't agree to go to the Holiday Ball with Felix, as you well know. I'm sorry, Felix."

Felix sneezed in her direction, still staring at her with hungry eyes and making her skin crawl like it was covered with centipedes. "What color is your dress?" he asked in the world's smarmiest voice. "I'll get boxers to match. Or briefs, if you like briefs."

"It's not happening. I have a date. I have a boyfriend." She glanced at Jay. He stepped right up to her side.

The words died on her lips, pointless and powerless because Felix simultaneously pronounced, "Boyfriend shmoyfriend. You promised me first." Felix grabbed at her, yanking her from Jay's side.

"I promised you nothing." She pulled her shoulder out of his grip.

"I'm sure you'll be changing your mind." Una Mae, her face smug, pulled an extra long pen from her snakeskin purse. "I only want both my son and you two to get what you want most. I'm motivated only by you young people's happiness." Una Mae smiled, squinting her eyes at Leela, whose skin crawled twice as much under the mother's gaze as under the son's.

"She has a date to the Holiday Ball." Jay tugged her back to his side. "Wherever it's held."

Clearly Jay wasn't committed to letting the ball—or the Cookie House—happen at the Layton Mansion.

All the little floating ships inside Leela sank.

"Yeah, wherever it's held," Leela squeaked, but then she steeled her voice. "Go ahead and sign, Jay. Your partnership at Precious Companion is waiting. I want you to find happiness. It's all I wish for you."

"You said you'd be *my* date to the Holiday Ball." Felix growled from his perch on the kitchen island. "You promised me first."

"Felix—" Leela shook her head at the oaf.

"Sign the documents, Jay!" Una Mae shouted, quelling Leela's retort to the angry son. "Felix, go outside. You promised to keep your emotions in check. We all keep our promises here, *right*?"

"I promised to clean out the attic." Jay placed his hands on his hips. "And if there's anything of value up there, it belongs to Layton family heirs."

Valuable things in the attic? What was that about? Had Leela missed something important?

"Ah, no." Una Mae backtracked all of a sudden. "That's not necessary. No delays of sale necessary. Fine. You can have your Cookie House promise. I'll allow it. Where do I add exceptions to the contract?" Una Mae waved her pen around. "Let's just get this in ink."

What? Una Mae was suddenly relenting on the Cookie House?

"Oh, Jay. Agree now!" Leela pressed him. "It's the best offer you're going to get." She'd find the decorations somewhere else other than the shed—apologies to Hildy's wishes—maybe even borrow

Rudolph, since Una Mae was changing her stripes.

That, or the other ladies in the Auxiliary would come through at the last moment.

"It lets you win. You can go to Reedsville."

"No." Jay's face hardened. "I inherited the house, and with it came explicit wishes from Uncle Jingo."

"To blazes with Jingo Layton!" Una Mae erupted, just as her phone rang, cutting her off mid-retort. "Excuse me."

Una Mae took the call in the other room, and Felix slunk away who knew where, giving Leela the chance to talk with Jay at last.

"What are you hesitating for, Jay? Take the money, get your partnership. Quick, while she's letting Cookie House stay alive. This way we all get to win."

"Do we? Do we really, Leela?" Jay looked hurt. "You want me to go?"

"I want you to have your dream."

"But—" Jay shook his head quickly. "No. We need to discuss that topic in greater depth. Soon. But for now, we have to put on the brakes." He lowered his voice and stepped closer, whispering. "Una Mae said some shocking things about your mother and mine while you were upstairs, and I have to tell you about them. However, for now, something else is even *more* urgent than that. I need to follow up on something that flew out of Felix's mouth a minute ago."

Leela cringed. "Ew."

"That didn't sound like I meant it to." Jay laughed, and the tension dispersed. "Quick, before Una Mae Coldicott comes back from her phone call. We need to check something in the attic."

"It's not a good time to make out." Leela followed him up the staircase. "But I did find something that might make the Cookie House a million times better."

"You found it?" Jay stopped and turned around, looking at her like she'd discovered gold.

"Do you even know what I'm talking about?" How could he know about Hildy's wishes and the glass décor?

"Of course I know about it. We found it together last week. It's amazing! If it's real, I mean."

None of this computed. She climbed after his quick ascent. "Huh? Dude, I'm talking about vintage Christmas decorations in the attic—and allegedly piles more in the shed. I found an old letter in the attic saying so."

"Vintage Christmas decorations. Okay." Jay nodded but he clearly had no idea how it mattered. "Cool?"

"Very cool, but not relevant to this moment, apparently. All right, since it's not that, then what are *you* talking about?"

They arrived at the top of the stairs and pushed their way into the dusty room where they'd spent so much time lately.

"Remember that big ceramic egg we found? Felix mentioned it cryptically, and Una Mae went berserk."

"The decorated one? Are you suggesting it's valuable?" Knock her over with a feather. "For more than just the gold filigree on its edges?"

"I don't really know." Jay resumed climbing the stairs, and Leela followed. "How much do you trust the word of Felix Coldicott?"

Leela stopped in her tracks. "As far as I can shove him." How far can a small woman shove an ocean liner?

"Exactly. But it's worth checking out. Maybe. Or a waste of time. I don't really know."

Leela must have missed a lot of conversational details while she was upstairs. What had Felix even said? "I think I remember where it was." She grabbed the ledger and found the box listed in the inventory.

Una Mae's boots clunked up the steps toward them, and she yoo-hooed for Jay and Leela.

"Delay her."

"Knowing the box number will help, but we didn't exactly put the boxes in any certain order when we finished with them." Rookie error.

"It will take too much time to find it."

"I'll stop her. But I want you with me as I do. Is that okay?"

So very okay. All the Os and all the Ks in the world. Times ten.

Jay took her hand and they descended the stairs together, to face the dragon lady. Oh, and her icky son.

Chapter 21

Jay

Una Mae saw them coming and continued up the stairway. "No need to meet in the kitchen. I'd love to see all the floors of the house. I've examined the second story thoroughly while the two of you dilly-dallied. What's in the attic?"

No way was Una Mae getting up into the attic. Not until he'd deciphered her intentions. "The attic is full of worthless knickknacks. Macramé crafts, soap-on-a-rope, the occasional piece of plastic fruit."

"Burt said you were in the process of an inventory."

Yeah, but if Una Mae thought she was getting a view of their list, she had another thing coming.

Leela stood shoulder-to-shoulder with him, creating a roadblock against Mrs. Coldicott's progress up to the attic. *Together we really do make an effective team.*

"I only need to check it for one little thing." She smiled in a way she must have thought sweetly, but it only seemed sinister. "Then, if you like, I'll consider upping my cash offer, since I'm asking for immediate occupancy."

"Mrs. Coldicott, I—"

"Don't say no, Dr. Wilson. Not until you've heard my offer. I believe it will be extremely tempting."

Leela squeezed his hand—hard. Almost like she was telling him he should consider it.

"Mother!" Felix called from the base of the stairway. Could four people logically be jamming themselves into this narrow passageway? "Mr. Basingstoke is back and wants to show you the paperwork. And I need my lunch soon."

Of course Felix did.

"Yes, sweetums. But Mother is checking something upstairs. The thing you like."

"Mother! Mr. Basingstoke is here." He stomped his foot, and it echoed up the stairwell. "He *told* me to come get you all. If we don't sign the paper, we don't get me a house."

Una Mae retreated a step, wobbling on a spiked heel but catching herself on the stair rail. "I'll be right there, sunshine." Finally, she peeled her gaze from Jay's and turned around.

Jay held Leela back as the Coldicotts retreated. *Something is definitely not right with those people.* When they were out of earshot, he whispered to Leela. "Thanks. I don't want them in the attic."

"You don't trust them either?"

Nope.

Jay descended, with Leela still holding his hand.

Downstairs, Burt would be waiting for signatures and a commission. Jay was going to owe Burt an explanation.

Chapter 22

Leela

In the kitchen, Burt and Una Mae stood beside the pile of hundred-dollar bills. How Jay could give them up, she still couldn't believe, but bless him for it. This house deserved Jay Wilson, not Felix Coldicott.

Jay kissed Leela on the temple, then left her side. "Burt, I need to talk to you privately."

"I'm through with private discussions!" Una Mae screeched and shoved a pen into Jay's hand. "This offer *will* expire, Jay Wilson. My patience is not infinite."

It had to be hot air. Didn't it? Leela held her breath, taking a step backward away from the battle zone.

She bumped right into the cologne-soaked Felix Coldicott.

"So, Leela." Felix placed a paw on her shoulder, sending a shudder up her neck. "So, my Leela. How is your father?"

The non sequitur jarred her. "What about my father?" Dad was not part of this discussion. "He's fine, thank you. His health is improving." That might or might not be true, but Dad was a fighter. He wasn't going to let the accident conquer his spirit.

"He'd be a lot *more* fine if he hadn't married your mother." Felix guffawed and rubbed his hands together. "My mama says so every day. Your mama, quote, ruined his potential. She made him go to work when

119

he could have had Mama's money and lived the life of a gentleman."

What on earth!

"What are you talking about, Felix?" Leela squirmed out of his grasp and wheeled around. His eye gleamed when his gaze landed on her. She took a step back, as if by instinct.

"Hush your gossiping mouth, Felix," Una Mae hissed.

Jay dropped the pen and strode toward Leela. "This isn't gossip, Leela. Una Mae admitted some of this herself while you were upstairs earlier."

"Are we signing this thing or not?" Burt asked.

Una Mae skittered over to Felix, pushing him toward the door. "Son, I think it's time you did a little exploration of your new home. Let's finish up that paperwork, Dr. Wilson. We're almost finished now."

A wave of pity roiled up from Leela's gut. Felix might not be all there. His lecherous gaze could be due to mental deficiency. The off-center comments, the leer in his eye, the obvious lack of social acumen—he couldn't be completely there.

"Felix, can you explain this to me?" she asked from a safe distance.

"No, Felix." Una Mae stood between Felix and the listeners.

He pushed his face over her shoulder. "*Your* mama stole Mr. Miller right out of my mama's grasp." His eye gleamed, like he was revealing something salacious. "She's not gonna forgive. She's not gonna forget."

Wait. What? Una Mae and Dad? Not even! Never! The mother was as delusional about romantic relationships as her son.

Felix pushed his mom aside, and she bumped against the wall. Felix stalked toward Leela. Jay stepped forward to stop Felix's progress, but Leela held out a hand. "I need to hear this."

"'Cause of all that, my mama isn't gonna let your mama have a seat at the Ladies' Auxiliary table ever again, not even if it's through you—*my Leela*." He stepped closer, his hot breath in her face. Leela retreated a pace reflexively. "You're really pretty, you know? Just like your mama. I saw her picture once."

He really wasn't all there. But his words still revealed the roots of Una Mae's vindictive crusade.

Leela rounded on Una Mae. "You're jealous of my mother? Is this why you've been bent on killing the Cookie House this year—because it was my mother's legacy? You planned to torpedo it all along. Then, when I was involved, you had to step up your game. Ruin it from a distance. And now by throwing money at the man I love. You'll stop at nothing, it seems."

"Felix imagines things." Alarm laced her tone.

Felix lunged for Leela. "You're gonna be mine. Mama promised."

"He imagines things?" Jay took Leela by the arm, leading her out of Felix's range of motion. "Like Fabergé eggs?"

"What are you talking about?" Leela had missed something important. Fabergé? She'd seen the egg upstairs, but no way was it an old Russian heirloom like a Fabergé. Not in Massey Falls. Russia was on the other side of the world.

Una Mae simmered like a pressure cooker's whose gauge gone way past the red line.

"This." Jay pulled out his phone and typed something in. He pulled up a picture and showed it to Leela. It was a pretty, decorative egg with gold filigree similar to the one they'd found upstairs.

"That's not a legend," Felix chanted. "That's not a myth. It's a truth. I saw it in a old newspaper. I told Mama about it just last night."

"Felix!" Una Mae strained. "I think it's time you went home."

"I read lots of old newspapers, guys. I'm not stupid."

"Burt"—Jay turned to the real estate agent—"you know much about antiques?"

"I see a lot of them during estate sales when properties are going on the market, but I'm not an appraiser. I've got a buddy in Torrey Junction who owns a shop and appraises professionally. He's a glass expert, but he has connections. Why?"

Leela started putting things together. The egg they'd found, the speed of the sale, the insistence on cleaning out the attic—all of Una Mae's strange behavior compounding into this crazy moment.

"Thanks, Felix. We appreciate your help."

"Felix!" Una Mae went into shrill mode. "Don't you remember our plan? We went over this. This was how we kill two birds with one stone—you get your expensive, pretty egg, and your girlfriend, and I get revenge on the girl who stole my boyfriend. Son! You like killing birds with stones."

Jay stepped toward Una Mae. "I can't sell the Layton Mansion—or the contents of the attic—to you. I'm sorry. And yes, the Cookie House will be held here."

Una Mae swallowed a noisy scream. "No, it won't. I won't let it. I don't care what the contingency says in the contract! If I lock the house, no one can bring cookies in. If I burn it down, all the better. It'll be mine. I can't be forced into it."

"You won't have a say."

"I'll still have a say on the Ladies' Auxiliary!" Una Mae yelled. "You, Leela Miller, won't be on the Ladies' Auxiliary board, you daughter of the woman who stole my one true love." Her eyes glittered with hot orange lava.

Leela grabbed Jay's elbow for support and solidarity against the madwoman. "All the notices have been printed. It's happening here."

Una Mae looked as if she might literally explode, with her head popping right off her body.

Felix patted his mother's shoulder. "It's okay, Mama. I'll kill you a different bird."

Jay took the sales contract and ripped it in half. "Take your cash."

Una Mae let out a stifled scream, then grabbed her pile of money and stomped out, slamming the front door hard enough to rattle all the windowpanes.

The storm was over. The sun was coming out. Burt shook his head. "I'll see you two later. Let me know if you still want to sell, son. I'll be glad to draw up another contract."

There was a reason that guy was the best real estate agent in Massey Falls. Nothing unnerved him. His sedan tore off down Society Row.

Jay laced his fingers through Leela's and led her out of the kitchen and into the grand ballroom, which she'd seen by peeking through the windows the first day she met Jay. It was so much grander from this perspective.

Leela trailed along beside Jay, across the parquet floors, her feet floating like they were made of helium.

He hadn't sold the house. He might stay. "I'm so glad this place didn't end up getting burned down by Una Mae Coldicott. You've done too much to restore its glory."

"It really is a great place. Especially when I see it through your eyes."

"Thanks for not selling to Una Mae." And maybe not to anyone else, please? *Please say you're not leaving Massey Falls, Jay. Don't go off to Reedsville. Not just when I'm starting to rely on you.*

"If what's upstairs is what Felix says, I think Dr. Harrison here in town might be getting a new partner in his large animal clinic."

"You mean that egg thing really could be valuable? It's not just Felix's freaky imagination?"

"I have a feeling it's extremely valuable. And if it is, I'll sell it … so that I can stay."

Stay. The most beautiful syllable in the universe.

Chapter 23

Jay

"Whoa, whoa. Be careful there." Jay rushed down the front steps of the Layton Mansion to grab two of the three trays Leela balanced in her arms. Each was piled high with cellophane and ribbon in dangerous-looking tufts. "Did you bake all these?"

Inside each transparent, crinkly bag lay a dozen perfectly round replicas of the cookies Leela had bewitched him with three weeks ago. Jay's mouth watered.

"They're still warm," she said. "Some are really warm. I hope they don't melt the cellophane."

"You may have wrapped them up, but I can still smell the ginger and cloves through the bags." The scent of the cookies infused all his senses.

"Good. And yes, I baked them, but Emily helped me."

Jay hadn't helped bake like he'd planned. Instead, he'd first been swamped with cutting ties with Foster & Cody. Then there were the final preparations inside the house and stringing ten thousand twinkle lights in the ballroom for the Holiday Ball. Add to that, his negotiation meetings with Overson and Harrison.

The future-maker men.

He couldn't wait to spring the news on Leela. But first she needed to bask in the transformation they'd accomplished in the house for this event, to take in its full effect.

"Emily will be here in a minute. Wow." Leela stepped through the front entrance, and Jay kept an eye on her face. "The room looks even better with the fire lit and glowing."

Just like her eyes. Mission accomplished.

Across the fireplace mantel were draped evergreen garlands and ribbons, each dripping with shiny vintage decorations that he and Leela had extracted from the loft in the shed. They'd also found candles, lanterns, old musical instruments, and a top hat that looked as if could have been worn by Charles Dickens himself.

"No trace of Rudolph or Misfit Toys here."

Under the direction of Leela's masterminding, stepping into the Layton Mansion was like stepping back to Victorian times.

Except with a much wider variety of cookies.

There were peanut butter blossoms with a chocolate kiss on top; lemon bars; chocolate crinkles with the powdered sugar coating; pumpkin drop cookies with chocolate chips and walnuts; pressed butter cookies in the shapes of holly leaves; scottish shortbread with decorative pinpricks; classic chocolate chip; and, for Jay, the crowning cookie: gingersnaps.

"There's no room for them all." Leela looked around, a look of dismay in her brows. Cookies already covered every available surface. He and Leela and a small army of Ladies' Auxiliary women had spent half the night placing everything just so. "I should have budgeted space for the gingersnaps."

"Check out this table I reserved just for your amazing cookies." Jay pointed to a table nestled to the side of the Christmas tree. Its ornate legs and finely carved apron fit the décor of the day.

"It's gorgeous." Leela ran a hand over the inlay surface, her tiny gasp sending a thrill up his spine.

"I found it behind a stack of boxes this morning." He slid it to a more prominent place in the room.

"It looks just like the banister."

Sure enough, she was right. It did match. The table looked to have been fashioned by the same craftsman as the rest of the house. This house was the gift that just kept on giving.

It gave me Leela.

"This table will host the first wave of gingersnaps." Jay held out the tray for her to offload her baked wares. "I know they'll sell."

"If I tell them it's my mom's recipe, they will." Leela unwound her scarf and took off her jacket. Jay took it to the coat closet. It looked natural hanging there, like it belonged.

"So, you went back up in the attic this morning? Weren't you tired after all the work I put you to?" Leela arranged her cellophane and ribbons just so.

"I was looking to see if the Fabergé egg we found had any twins up there." They'd had it appraised, and they learned that Jay was the owner of a true, imperial egg that had been missing from public knowledge for fifty years. "I heard a rumor of a second one."

"Was there?" Leela's eyes grew wider than the egg's circumference. "That's too much to imagine."

"No, no second egg. But I do have good news." This was the moment he'd been waiting for. He'd just solidified details of the deal this morning. He'd been waiting to see Leela in person to spring it on her—and watch how she'd take the announcement. "Dr. Harrison is willing to take the Fabergé egg in exchange for the buying price of his veterinary practice."

"Seriously?" Leela ran and threw herself into his arms, nearly knocking him backward. He lifted her up and swung her around, barely missing a cookie display. "He's trading it to you? For the egg?"

"More or less. We're still ironing out his exit plan. He's not ready to retire just yet."

Leela shook her head, her eyes bright and blinking. "That's amazing. But wait a minute. Isn't the business still worth much more than the egg?"

He set her down, and they laced fingers together. "Probably. I don't know." So much depended on auctions. "The fact is, Dr. Harrison loves them with an obsession."

"Seriously?"

"Yeah, apparently, he had a Russian ancestor, and now that he's a veterinarian for farm animals—it makes the egg a perfect crossroads as a collectible. He gets what he values—and so do I."

Leela's eyes shone. "What do you value, Jay?"

Jay enfolded her again. Jay looked around the Layton Mansion. Its value had certainly risen in his own eyes since he'd first taken possession of it. Not only the value he'd added by remodeling it, but the value Leela added by loving it—and by showing him a vision of what it could be like.

Also, the scent of cookies didn't hurt.

"Me? What do I value? The house. This place. And the people who love it as much as I do."

"Jay, this is just so—Oh, my goodness!" Leela looked at the pendulum clock on the mantel. "The Cookie House opens its doors in fewer than five minutes!"

What had she been going to say? It didn't matter. Jay had a feeling there would be ample time to explore this topic of conversation in days to come. Maybe even tonight when she was his date for the Holiday Ball.

She was going to love what he'd done with the ballroom.

"Five minutes? Good. I'm starved." Jay tugged at the ribbon on a bag and began to reach inside. "I'll pay for these cookies as soon as the cash box is here, but I can't wait another second. The siren song of the molasses is luring me toward the rocks."

"Jay! Shouldn't you wait?"

"What for? I've been waiting." For all of this. For too many years. He took his first sugar-crystal-coated bite. "Mmm. You are a goddess in the kitchen." And in the attic, as well as on a loveseat in front of a fire.

Leela's sweetness had him addicted.

A car's engine sounded out front, and several Ladies' Auxiliary members trouped up the walk, chattering. They gasped when they entered.

"Oh, Leela Miller! It's just as beautiful as when your mother first began this event." Mrs. Imrich came and put an arm around Leela's shoulders. "She would be so proud. I'm sure she's with you here today."

Mrs. Philbert humphed. "Much classier than all those stupid cartoon reindeer we've had the last few years." She pulled some money out of her purse. "Now, I'll take three plates of Freesia's gingersnaps."

Chapter 24

Leela

Within minutes of the ladies' arrival, a string of cookie-hungry shoppers lined the stairways, the hallways, the kitchen, and all three floors. Some had brought shopping baskets and were already filling them to the brim.

"I haven't made neighbor gifts for years. I just use cookies from the Cookie House." The first shopper handed Leela a wad of cash. "But I always save two bags of these for myself." She held two bags of gingersnaps to her heart. "I miss your mother, Leela. It's so good you could fill her shoes."

A pang went through Leela, and her eyes prickled. "No one could fill Mom's shoes. But I can bake her cookies."

"She's in your heart, honey."

The day went on, and tray after tray of cookies made their way out the door. The money in the till had to be taken to the bank twice, for safe-keeping, due to the staggering amount. Even a very-pregnant Natalie came through, having broken away from wedding events at Yuletide Manor to come and get cookies. She'd hugged Leela, popped a ginger snap in her mouth, and hustled back to the Hawthorn family's celebrations.

"I swear, there are five times as many people buying cookies this year compared to last year." Emily plopped two plates of lemon bars onto the sale table where Leela took a turn toward the end of the sale day. "I think it's because they wanted to peek inside the Layton Mansion. Just like you. Remember when you broke the house that first night you met Jay?" She strung Jay's name out to several syllables, batting her eyelashes. "I know you're in love with Jay." Again with the extra-long *Jay*.

Of course, Jay walked up at that second. "Do I hear my name?"

Impeccable timing. "Emily just reminded me I never repaired the wood slat from the window frame I broke the night we met. I still plan to pay for that."

"I already took payment." He wiped a few dark brown crumbs off the front of the dark red Henley shirt that emphasized his build. "In cookies."

Emily grinned. "She only started making *good* cookies once she met you, you know." Her snicker echoed off the high ceiling. "I'm excited to see you two at the Holiday Ball in a few hours. Leela, you're going to love my dress, and I can't wait to see yours! With you in Jay's arms." She took her lemon bars and sashayed, as if already dancing at the Holiday Ball. "At least I'll try to notice you two, even though I'll be swooning over Aiden Ryerson. Don't forget you're going to do my hair, Leela." She spun once before leaving the room.

The next woman in line winked. "Forgive me for eavesdropping, but I must say, you two will be the prettiest couple at the prettiest Holiday Ball this town has ever seen. I peeked into the ballroom—and it's heaven. You've outdone even your mother's highest aspirations, Leela. We're all so impressed with what you've done. And she would be, too. And I can tell this young man is impressed as well. He's got *smitten* written all over his face."

Leela glanced up at him, and he didn't look the least bit shy about the accusation. He responded with that dangerously handsome grin, and then he melted into the crowd while Leela helped the customers in the line.

It was nice just knowing he was around supporting her.

When the traffic at her cash box let up, he reappeared. "I've been over at your house."

"My house?"

"I thought your dad would like to see your work."

"Dad!" Leela shut her cash box. "He's coming? Here?" She stood up. She had to help him. The snow, the ice—he could slip, and—

"He's sitting near the fire in the parlor, acting a hundred percent at home. I took him around to see the remodeling I'd done."

"He was okay walking in the snow?"

"He needed a little help."

Which probably meant a lot of help. "Oh, Jay. Thank you for bringing him." What an incredibly thoughtful gesture. "I'm sure he loves what you've done with the place."

"In his own way, he let me know."

Dad could definitely do that. "Thank you." Leela went up on tiptoe and kissed Jay's cheek. A smattering of stubble pricked against her upper lip. "I can't thank you enough."

"Ah! I saw that!" Emily came up, sniggering. "Save it for after the Holiday Ball, guys. Kiss under the mistletoe at midnight like you're supposed to." She made kissing sounds and mashed her hand against her mouth. "At least that's what I'm going to do with Aiden Ryerson."

Burt Basingstoke roared up. "Oh, no, you're not." He took Emily's elbow and guided her out the front door.

Time would prove whether father or daughter was correct.

More cookie sales followed, and Jay helped Dad get home after Leela sat with him a few minutes by the fire. He seemed so at ease. It was comforting.

Too bad Jay's mom hadn't come to see today's beautiful event. Maybe someday.

The final plate of cookies sold, and the clock struck four. Jay shut the front door. "Cookie sales for the Christmas Cookie House are officially completed."

"Everyone gather in the kitchen," Leela called up the stairs and down the hallways to the remaining volunteers. A scant half-dozen plates of cookies remained—rice crispy bars, coffee-flavored cookies, peanut butter blossoms, and a couple of chocolate chip plates. "I have napkins, cups, and milk."

"In all our years, we've never once come this close to selling out all the cookies." Mrs. Imrich of the Ladies' Auxiliary carried a load of empty trays down the stairs from the second floor. "I am amazed, since we had even more bakers than usual. Although I shouldn't be amazed. The Layton Mansion brought them in. You were right, Leela. This was the perfect place. And thank you, Dr. Wilson. You made our whole year's work possible, and then some! People loved your house."

"You're welcome." He pulled Leela to his side, pressing her hip against his own. His warmth soaked through her on this cold third-Tuesday-in-December. "I did it for Leela."

The room disappeared, and so did the cookie crumbs and the ladies. It was just Leela and her beating heart and Jay's admission for a moment.

He did it for me.

"Yes, Leela. Of course, we will love to induct Leela into the society at our next meeting. She's more than proven herself worthy of skipping the one-year probationary period. But be careful, if you continue to succeed on this level, you'll end up being the president in no time."

And supplant Una Mae? "I don't know. There are some people who really like, you know, being in charge."

As if reading Leela's mind, Mrs. Imrich lowered her voice and said, "Maybe so, but sometimes they *charge* the rest of us too much with their personalities. I'm supporting you for the new officer election. I hope you'll accept the nomination."

New officer! Even Mom hadn't aspired to leadership positions in the Ladies' Auxiliary. She'd quietly served, not putting herself in the spotlight, just being the workhorse instead of the show pony, coming up with fundraising ideas, and making them a reality. "I'll think about it."

Jay stepped up beside Leela. "She may have other commitments."

Leela's head snapped up, and she looked at him. "Oh?"

"We can discuss them at the Holiday Ball." Seeing his grin produced that bone-melting quality in Leela again. "Now, don't we have some rearranging to do here in the Layton Mansion so that the orchestra can fit in this room before the Holiday Ball can begin?"

Chapter 25

Jay

Strains of "Walking in a Winter Wonderland" wafted through the air of Jay's house. The orchestra played from the nether reaches of the ballroom, but the song filled all of the first floor with the holiday love song. Guests of all ages streamed in through the front doors in wool wraps and their best party gowns and suits. Members of the Ladies' Auxiliary directed them to the refreshments and the dance floor.

Other than the decorations, which were complete, Leela wasn't in charge of this portion of the day, thank goodness. Jay could have her attention all to himself, first on the ballroom floor with the beautiful girl in his arms, and then he intended to just sit quietly with her in front of the fire—with no cookies.

For now, Jay couldn't tear his eyes away from the stairway. The banister he'd so diligently sanded, stained, and varnished in the summer finally had a sight worthy of gracing it because the incredible Leela Miller descended the stairs in a long, green velvet gown.

Her light brown hair flowed around her shoulders in soft curls, and a ruby sparkled on a black ribbon choker at her throat.

"Jay, you look like a Victorian gentleman." Leela glided down like a swan in flight and took his arm. "I think your forebears would be impressed."

Jay knew *he* was impressed. Every inch of Leela was making a serious impression on him right now. "You did it. All of it."

"Now, wait a minute. Who helped me unearth the candlesticks in the attic? Who climbed into the rafters of the shed to get down the Victorian Christmas ornaments? Who stood on the ladder and draped garlands from chandelier to chandelier? And those twinkle lights as numerous as the stars in the sky?"

"That guy wouldn't have done it but for you." Jay took her hand, lacing her fingers between his. He took her to the front room where the Christmas tree stood tall and straight, its star on top grazing the plaster of the ceiling. "Is it close to what you envisioned when you were Emily's age?"

"It's much, much better."

"Shall we make our entrance into the ballroom?"

"It's a little cold." She shivered as guests streamed in through the front entrance, each bringing in some of the winter night with them. "Can we stand beside the fire? Maybe by the fire in the parlor?"

Yes, his thoughts were her thoughts, it would seem. He led her through the hallway to the parlor of the back bedroom. "Your dad looked pretty cozy here earlier."

"Quite. I talked to him a little while ago at home. He said something like fireplace, and smiled." They entered the warm room. "A fireplace is something our house definitely lacks. He'd benefit from one, I believe."

Well, he could have one here, if things went the way Jay hoped.

The flame beckoned, warm and glowing orange, the only light in the dim but inviting room. He led her to a loveseat which was placed near the hearth, and sat down beside her.

"This is nice," she said. "Can we stay here a bit? We have all night to dance."

They had all their lives to dance, if things kept going the way he felt them heading tonight. The Layton Mansion could host their own family Christmas gatherings—for years to come. Leela had first given him a glimpse of that vision on this very loveseat, and since then, it had expanded to a grander, multi-generational saga of happiness, laughter, and beauty.

Leela settled in beside him on the couch, sliding off her shoes and lifting her feet onto the ottoman, nearer the fire.

"Dr. Harrison has his attorney drawing up paperwork." Jay wrapped a tendril of Leela's hair around his fingertip. While Leela prepared for the dance, Jay had been mapping his next career move. And it didn't involve moving anywhere, except permanently to Massey Falls.

"Already?"

"He's anxious to get his hands on the prize." Just like Jay was.

"It's funny, isn't it?" She leaned her head against his chest, locking into a perfect fit in his arms. "You had a deadline today for signing to purchase a place in a veterinary clinic. You just didn't know you'd end up signing papers to be the next large animal vet in Massey Falls."

Dr. Harrison would be interesting to work with until he retired in a year or two. Jay still had a lot to learn, and Dr. Harrison seemed anxious to show him. Plus, Jay would get to practice the type of veterinary medicine he loved most, and Whitmore Thoroughbreds even offered him a position as their track-side vet for future races at Torrey Stakes.

"Things sometimes don't work out the way you think, but they end up being a whole lot better." He pressed a kiss into her hair.

"Burt bumped into me today when he came through to buy cookies. He probably just wants to know if he can count on the listing. He knows you're not selling to Una Mae, understandably, but he wants to know—are you going to sell the Layton Mansion?" A tightness tugged in her voice.

Couldn't she see where he'd been headed with all this *stay in Massey Falls* stuff? He'd better make his intentions clearer—even if it meant moving things at a faster pace than most guys would deem prudent. "Well, I can't very well sell the Layton Mansion now."

"What do you mean?" Leela pulled out from beneath his arm and curled around to look at him. "Why not sell? It's so valuable. Think what you could do with that windfall."

"The truth is"—he cupped her chin with his hand— "you've shown me its real value."

Her eyes softened. "And what is that?"

"As a place for a family."

"Whose"—her voice trembled—"family would that be, Jay?"

"Well, my own, for starters." Jay traced a circle on the back of Leela's hand. "I did what you asked."

"What did I ask?"

"I called my mom. I invited her to see the house. Sent a few snapshots over the phone."

"Oh?" Leela's breath bated. "And?"

"And she said she'd think about it. She said it looked like a lot of junk had been cleared out, and that maybe it was time to clear out some of her own junk. Actually, she got especially interested when I told her we'd found the journal. And that I had met someone special in Massey Falls."

"Did you mean … me?" He'd mentioned her? "Does she know I'm Freesia's daughter?"

"I think I'll spring that on her later."

Good plan. "You said, *for starters*." Leela didn't want to press— but she wanted to press. "What family do you have in mind for this house after the *starters*?"

"Let me draw you a mental picture." He described the rooms, the way they could fill them, with her father, their children, her baking projects, their large dog, their future lives together.

"I can see it, too, Jay. Plain as the firelight."

"Good." He pressed a kiss to her forehead, letting his lower lip linger on her soft skin. "You recall, when that woman asked you to take over the Ladies' Auxiliary, I mentioned you might have other commitments." He pressed a kiss to her temple.

"I recall." Leela's eyes fluttered shut, and he pressed a kiss upon the lid of her left eye, and then upon her right, eliciting a sigh. "Like what?"

He'd like to elicit a lot more sighs, just like that one. "Like, for instance, being my precious companion." To which she giggled, and he kissed her mouth softly, teasing her into a return kiss, warm like the fire he'd built for them. "And sharing raw cookie dough with me, right off the spoon." He kissed her again. "And building a future family here, with kids sliding down banisters, and a dog or two, and singing around the fireplace—as my wife?"

"Those are commitments I feel completely ready to make," she promised with a kiss of sugar and spice.

Epilogue

Bing Whitmore

Bing Whitmore stomped toward the stables, the gravel crunching beneath his work boots. "It's not about the loss of income, Freya."

Yes, he should have developed thicker skin for this business by now, but when Rose Red's leg broke, it nearly broke Bing in the same complex fracture.

Yes, horse breeding and racing were risky ventures, and getting too attached to individual horses increased the risk exponentially, but the problem was, Rose Red's fracture followed hot on the heels of losing million-dollar Torrey Stakes winner Snow White just that summer.

"You love the horses." Freya double-stepped to catch up with him. "More than anything or anyone. I get that, Bing." His cousin brushed the collecting snowflakes off her shoulders. "We all do. It's in our Whitmore blood."

"Then you get why I need to quit." Quit horses. Quit all of it.

"Quit! Owners don't quit."

"They do if they sell their shares of the business to the other partners."

"But, Bing! You're the one who runs the day-to-day aspects of Whitmore Stables. The rest of us are owners because of Grandpa, but we're not exactly involved, not like you are."

"Well, the you can hire someone to replace me. A professional." Someone who wouldn't go Three-Mile Island every time he picked up a curry comb to clean off a dusty flank or smelled leather. "Lots of guys out there would kill for a chance to manage a stable full of thoroughbreds."

"Bing." Freya slid her glasses off her head and balanced them on the end of her nose. "What's really going on here?"

Uh-oh. It never worked in his favor when Freya started using her PhD in psychology on him. "I don't need any head-shrinking, not even with the family discount."

"Is this about the surgery? Rose Red is getting better."

But she'd never race again, although at least she was alive. If that rookie veterinarian hadn't shown up, Bing would have lost Rose Red, too.

And then what? Bing would have wandered off into the snow-covered hills with just the clothes on his back and become a statistic.

"Fine. No head-shrinking. And I can see you're not going to answer any of my probing, empathetic questions—so I'll just give you some unsolicited advice."

Which he would reject, obviously.

"Don't quit. Or sell. Or whatever. Not today."

Maybe tonight, then. "It's best for Whitmore Stables, Frey."

"What about a vacation?"

"People in my line don't take vacations." Animal care wasn't the kind of thing that could just be put on hold. The horses needed food, exercise, and close supervision. "In my eight years at Whitmore, I haven't missed a day."

"That's what I'm talking about." Freya punched his upper arm. "You need a break. Maybe some easygoing socialization with humans instead of animals. You've been through a lot this summer and fall. It's going to be rough on anyone."

No kidding. He crossed his arms over his chest. And he wasn't getting into dating, if that was what Freya was hinting with her *easygoing socialization* verbiage.

They stood at the door of the stables, the wind howling and the snow collecting.

"Fine. Say you did quit, walk away from this—that would be a permanent vacation. You might not like it. Did you think of that? How about just giving it a trial run first? Just like you'd do with the horses, practice runs before a race."

Bing shut his eyes. Freya would gloat if he agreed she was making sense.

"Honestly, I wouldn't even know how to take a vacation."

"Look, I'll talk to Dr. Harrison, see if he has someone he can recommend to man the stables for a few days"—she hiccuped when she must have seen his face—"make that *weeks*. Then, I'll look around online for a good vacation spot and book you something completely quiet. A hotel with nobody else even staying in it. Maybe in the mountains somewhere like Steamboat Junction or Wilder River. You used to ski when we were kids. Remember?"

This wouldn't work. Going away wouldn't make him want to come back. However, being in the mountains might give him some peace. "I totally beat you down that black diamond run."

"Ha! That was the beginners' hill and you know it."

"But the story is better my way."

"So you'll do it? I'm a great sleuth when it comes to finding off-the-beaten-path vacation spots. Not that I ever go to them, but this will be my big chance."

"You're going, too?" A little company might not hurt, instead of going everywhere alone in a strange place. "Uh, okay."

Freya pulled off her glasses. "You'll do it? I can make the plans?"

"Like you said, a trial run." But his gut said he was through with horses forever.

To read the rest of Bing's journey to love and healing at Christmastime, check out The Sleigh Bells Chalet, *Book 2 in the Christmas House Romance Series.*

BONUS RECIPE
from the Griffith family

Truly the Most Delicious Soft Gingersnaps In the World

These are the best cookies at the holidays—they taste like Christmas smells. Some call them molasses cookies, but my wonderful mother in law called them soft gingersnaps. Warning, they're addictive.

1 ½ cups butter
2 eggs
2 tsp ground cloves
1 ½ tsp salt
2 cups sugar
4 cups flour
2 tsp ginger
2/3 cup molasses
2 tsp cinnamon
4 tsp soda

Cream sugar and butter. Add eggs and molasses. Mix. Sift dry ingredients and add. Mix. Roll into 1 ½" balls and roll in granulated sugar. Bake 325° 10-12 minutes. Makes 5-6 dozen.

The Christmas House Romance Series

Yuletide Manor*
The Christmas Cookie House
The Sleigh Bells Chalet
The Holiday Hunting Lodge
Peppermint Drop Inn

*Free full-length e-novel with baking and Christmastime romance in beautiful, snowy Massey Falls. Available exclusively to newsletter subscribers. Email jennifergriffithauthor@yahoo.com and ask for a link to this free book.

About the Author

Jennifer Griffith is the *USA Today* bestselling author of over forty novels and novellas. Two of her novels have received the Swoony Award for best secular romance novel of the year. She lives in Arizona with her husband, who is a judge and her muse. They are the parents of five children, which makes everyday life a romantic comedy. Connect with Jennifer via her website at authorjennifergriffith.com, where you can sign up for her newsletter to receive exclusive content and notices of new releases.

Made in the USA
Las Vegas, NV
07 December 2022

61422885R00090